THE DAYS A[...]

Migumi was sittin[...]
sake for me. He[...]
revealing her thigh[...] [...]aised
it to my lips. T[...] invigorated me
immediately and I began to feel excited. The
Japanese girl's thighs gleamed in the soft light.
She smelled of musk and now her hands were
resting on my knees. She looked directly at me
with her flashing eyes and said, 'Let me show
you the secret of my hospitality . . .'

Also available

THE FRENCH COLLECTION
INDISCREET MEMOIRS
LAURE-ANNE: THE COMPLETE CON-
FESSIONS
JOY
JOY AND JOAN
JOY IN LOVE
PLEASURES OF LOVING
PLAISIR D'AMOUR
JOIE D'AMOUR
FOLIES D'AMOUR
THE LIFTED CURTAIN
THE PLEASURES OF LOLOTTE
VIOLETTE
PARISIAN FROLICS
DREAMS OF FAIR WOMEN

THE DAYS
AND NIGHTS
OF MIGUMI

P. M.

*Translated from the French
by Alan Shipway*

A STAR BOOK
published by
the Paperback Division of
W.H. Allen & Co. PLC

A Star Book
Published in 1988
by the Paperback Division of
W.H. Allen & Co. Plc
44 Hill Street, London W1X 8LB

Typeset by Phoenix Photosetting, Chatham
Printed in Great Britain by
Cox & Wyman Ltd, Reading

ISBN 0 352 32090 7

THE DAYS AND NIGHTS OF MIGUMI

Chapter 1

The Les Halles district was deserted. I had made up my mind to go home. It was getting dark and a thick fog enveloped figures chilled by the gloomy winter. Entering the Rue de Turbigo, I saw a woman gathering up the provisions which had just fallen from her heavily overloaded basket. I started to help her.

She turned to me and said, 'Oh thank you, it's nothing serious, I can manage.'

'Have you got far to go? I'll walk with you, if you like. I'm going in the same direction anyway.'

'Well, I live in the Rue Tiquetonne.'

'What a coincidence! So do I.'

She was a young Japanese woman with her hair done in the style of Louise Brooks. She was wearing a very sophisticated coat, with extremely wide sleeves and geometric pockets. Her smile had made me forget about the cold. She thanked me repeatedly, assured me that we would soon be at her flat, and said how embarrassed she was to put me to so much trouble.

She invited me into her flat.

She turned on the lights, and I carried her provisions into the kitchen.

The moment my hands were free, I wondered what I was going to do.

'Please,' she said, 'let me offer you a cup of tea. I'm sure you could do with one.'

'Yes,' I replied.

She took me into the sitting room and turned on the light. There were green plants all around the room, big framed fashion plates hung on the walls and some erotic drawings were to be seen by a small bookcase.

I could hear her moving about in the kitchen. I took my coat off and sank down on to a black leather divan. Suddenly, I had the distinct impression that I was at home. But a home which had been entirely renewed; sensual, fresh, free. An odour of incense floated between those walls, and gradually the scent of tea mingled with it in the sitting room. I sensed a rustling of clothes; undoubtedly, she was undressing. She appeared in a kimono, a smile on her lips.

'I don't want to take up too much of your time,' I said.

'That is of no importance. We shall drink our

tea. Then I must prepare a meal for a friend who is coming at nine o'clock. I shan't keep you long.'

She came back from the kitchen carrying a tray on which stood a teapot and two white cups with a black monogram.

She served me, and as she bent forward, her kimono gaped open and I saw two little breasts with dark points. Her body was graceful, her movements alert and measured.

She came and sat beside me on the divan. 'My name is Migumi, you can call me Lili as all my French friends do,' she said. 'What's yours?'

'Patrick, that's not very French either . . . He's the patron saint of Ireland.'

'How cosmopolitan we are. I'm Japanese but my mother is Chinese, from Hong Kong. I've been working in France for some years in fashion and publicity.'

'Do you do photos?'

'Less, nowadays. I choose the models, I concern myself with collections. But I began with photography, then I decided to design and launch a new line. Now I direct a model agency.'

The telephone rang. She excused herself and went to answer it. It seemed to me that she was speaking Japanese. She looked a bit put out for a moment, then began to laugh. I didn't understand a word.

She hung up, then told me it was her friend, who wouldn't be coming to dinner after all.

'And after I've gone to so much trouble to prepare a nice meal. Never mind, I hereby invite you to a genuine Japanese meal! I hope that you are not expected elsewhere?'

'No, I accept with pleasure, Migumi. What a charming name!'

'I have other charms too,' she replied, as she disappeared into the kitchen.

I burst out laughing. It seemed to me that the evening was taking an exotic turn: I wasn't complaining. I knew a little about Japanese food, but nothing whatsoever about Japanese women. Nothing could please me more than to get to know the hidden aspect of the eastern woman. I recalled several books, a few films where eroticism is carried to a paroxysm, but all that was as yet nothing but a fantasy.

She came back again. I stood up and took my jacket off, for the flat was very warm. She took the garment from me and went to hang it up.

'If you would like to make yourself more comfortable, I have a kimono for you. Then you will not perspire; the house is heated to the point where one could live almost naked. Would you like some sake?'

'Please. But I'll go and change first.'

She showed me to her bedroom where I found a kimono in red silk and some wooden sandals. I undressed, retaining only my sweatshirt and my underpants. I put on the sandals, *getas*, which were very comfortable. I really did feel at home.

I returned to the lounge where she was sitting on the divan waiting for me with a glass of sake. Her legs were crossed, partly revealing her thighs. I took the glass and raised it to my lips. The sake reinvigorated me immediately, and I felt my sex grow erect after the first mouthful. Her thighs gleamed in the soft light. She kept bustling around the low table and the divan, brushing against me with her kimono. She was looking for a lighter for the perfumed candle. I offered her mine. She lit it, and handing it back to me, let it fall between my legs. She went to considerable trouble to try to find it again, and so did I. She made me separate my feet, telling me not to move. She found it.

My sex grew harder still. She smelled of musk and her hands were resting on my knees. She looked directly at me without any embarrassment whatever, her eyes were flashing.

'You're exciting in this kimono. I sense that you're rigid underneath it. I'm going to let you into the secret of my hospitality.'

I took her hand, but she withdrew it quickly and pushed my arms aside.

13

'Close your eyes, don't move. This is an extra aperitif.'

I closed my eyes and lay back comfortably on the divan. She undid the belt of the kimono, and I felt her hands drawing my prick out of my underpants. It stood up between her fingers. I was aware of her warm breath approaching. Her tongue lapped the tip of the glans quickly and repeatedly. Suddenly, she stopped. Now Migumi's tongue was licking my prick slowly, unlike before, and she maintained a motion which was extremely lazy and sweet. That slowness electrified my whole body. She tongue-fluttered with an expertise which was almost ceremonial. Then her hand grasped my prick. I heard her drink from the glass of sake. And before I realised what was happening, her tongue formed a liana, a creeper wrapped around my sex which she sucked in as though she wished to drain my life away. I felt I was in a hot, burning jungle, where undulating and fantastic plants were lacerating me with inconceivable caresses.

Colours, perfumes and sounds danced in my head. Lying there in the depths of the divan, I felt the sap of pleasure rising from the depths of my body. I put my hands on her ebony hair to precipitate my orgasm.

I gave a long and vibrant cry.

She sucked me to the last groan, swallowing

all of my sperm. The sake in her mouth had made my sex as hot and hard as a steel bar. She withdrew her head from between my thighs and gave me a radiantly happy smile.

'It was the effect of the sake which surprised you?'

'A bit, but more your skill. It's unforgettable.'

'I hope you have enough energy for the dessert.'

'But I shouldn't like . . .'

'No. Not now. I'm going to prepare you a sukiyaki and Japanese vegetable fritters. And we shall continue to drink sake.'

'I feel like a prince . . .'

'Don't worry, the princess is demanding! Meanwhile, I'll put some music on. Let me get on with my little dishes, make yourself at home. I shall be a few minutes, my prince!'

She had set up a low table which occupied a corner of the room. Little bowls of sauce, a dish of vegetables, and chopsticks were set out for the two of us. This part of the room was marked off by two sorts of Japanese screens. These were made of fairly thick paper stretched across a kind of frame of light wood.

As I kept staring at them, she said: 'They're called *shoji*. Most Japanese houses are full of them. I ordered these specially from Tokyo.

15

You can get them in Paris, but they're not so well-made.'

Butterflies, and cherry trees were painted on the *shoji*, a river flowed and children danced.

Migumi invited me to follow her example and eat with the chopsticks. She was surprised by my dexterity. She poured me some sake, and we drank a toast to our meeting.

'Your cooking is delicious,' I said.

'Thank you. I've remembered my grand-mother's recipes; she was a great cook in Tokyo. From time to time I try to honour her memory. It's not always easy with the life I lead! But when exceptional or unexpected circumstances arise, I turn to the traditions and give pleasure to those around me.'

'It's rarely that one meets a woman like you who concerns herself with keeping alive the traditional pleasures of living. It would be more likely to see you in a chrome-grey jump-suit like they wear in electrical components factories.'

'Oh, not at all! Technical progress is one thing, but I have remained essentially a *woman*! I like to take care of myself and to give myself completely to a man who likes that. You know, the Japanese are still torn between tradition and the hypermodernism of their society. Some of them have repudiated the past but others are still receptive to a certain art of

16

living. On the one hand it's whisky, on the other it's rice-alcohol.'

'But, these last few years, your country has developed considerably as far as manners and morals are concerned. There are public places such as the famous bars where the waitresses are topless, then, if you're in the mood, they're willing to pose bottomless in a private room.'

'It's westerners, Americans, who've brought about this state of affairs . . . It was an opportunity for certain Japanese businessmen to create a new version of exotic tourism and to reactualise the folklore of Japanese prints and geishas. But you haven't said what you think of this dish, is it to your liking?'

'Your little rissoles are excellent!'

'Rice, mint, garlic, and mushrooms, which I sauté.'

'It's quite highly seasoned. You've put some pepper in too.'

'Very little. It's the sake which produces that effect. Anyway, we have to finish the bottle before dessert.'

She arose from her *tatami* and went into the kitchen. For the second time, I saw the little points of her breasts. Black. Taut. Like choc-ices demanding to be sucked. A little while ago, she had left me unsatisfied. I wanted to take her in my arms, to mould her to my body, to bite her, to make her come totally.

I wondered what she had in store for me for the rest of the evening. I was anxious to be finished with this dinner, charming though it was.

She came back from the kitchen with some fruit. There were mangoes and a bowl filled with lychees in a rosy juice. She picked up a mango, cut it down the centre, pulled the two pieces apart and removed the stone.

'Here, use one of the little spoons, you'll find it easier that way.'

Her manners pleased me tremendously. She was a real mistress. While I was sampling the mango, I was already imagining my next ceremony with her. But I was far from foreseeing what she would demand of me at the end of that dainty meal.

Migumi poured me a final glass of sake.

She parted her kimono to the limit of her brown nipples, with geometrical precision, and said, 'I should like you to finish your drink, then I shall remain seated, and you can give me my extra aperitif. I want to be sucked.'

I moved the little table which was between us to one side and approached her.

The subtle light from the candles surrounded our two silhouettes with shadows. I pushed the folds of the kimono back from her thighs and slid my hands over her hips. I tipped her back slightly and passed my hands under her buttocks. She was as light as a feather, and it took little effort to lift her. I raised her sex to the level of my face. A heady perfume of musk and cinnamon rose from it. My tongue ran around her black and glossy hair. I turned my attention to the lips of her sex, which were slightly parted, and went all around them, making her groan suddenly. She was hot, burning. My tongue foraged between her lips, exploring her, gradually working towards the clitoris. I licked her from top to bottom, then from bottom to top with a slowness, which made me think of when, as a child gourmet, I used to secretly feast on little pots of chocolate fondant.

She began to get very agreeably wet. She tasted of vanilla cream. I penetrated deeper and deeper, then I concentrated on the surface. Her clitoris was becoming more clearly defined. I could feel it better. She gave another moan of pleasure to indicate that I had found her sensitive spot. I set her back down on the *tatami*, spread her thighs, and got right in between them. My mouth was moulded to that sex with its heady odours. I nibbled her from time to time, which drew unintelligible words from her. I no longer comprehended anything. My head was ringing with a strange sound. The more I caressed her, the stiffer I grew. She was twisting and turning all over the place. I was trying to hold her still. Her arms were thrown back behind her head, and sometimes she arched her back violently. Suddenly, she pulled her knees right back to her chest. I raised her buttocks again to bring her sex to my mouth.

I took her clitoris between my teeth. At that point, she cried out and gripped my head with her hands. I nibbled it gently, and I used my tongue intermittently as well. I thrust it in deep, then slowed down for a while. I would get my breath back and then go on nibbling again and again. It was driving me mad with pleasure. It seemed to me that her body was totally in harmony with mine. Her predisposition towards pleasure was without equal. I felt that I had known Migumi for years. That's very rare with chance meetings. But this evening was an exceptional case, absolutely sensational.

She made her excitement last to the point where she was almost delirious. She was now thrusting her sex at me as if she wanted to engulf my entire head. Suddenly, I increased the pressure on her clitoris, rolling it around between my teeth. Liquid was running down between her thighs. She tightened their grip on my head, squeezing me convulsively in a last explosive gasp.

I felt her melting, liquefying: all her muscles

relaxed, in that light her face looked like an angel's. My mouth was still warm from that palpitating body. She turned over on to her stomach. I kissed the plump, round buttocks which were thus exposed to me.

She looked up at me. 'Your dessert was quite devastating.'

'I was simply guided by your starter, and by the sake.'

'I love the sensation of sake on my vulva. Your tongue electrified me from the first moment.'

I smiled nonchalantly. But she left me no time for respite. One of her little feet was tickling my damp sex, from which a few drops of my excitation were appearing.

We were still in our kimonos. It seemed to me that we had been there for hours, although this impromptu evening had barely started.

I was continuing to caress her buttocks, when she said, 'I can see that you're still *hot*! We'll try something different now. Pick up that pot of almond cream which is on the table. It's still warm, I think.'

I obeyed without hesitation. She dipped a finger into the cream, then put it between her buttocks. I took the cream and started to grease her anus. Without any hesitation she made me introduce my finger into her.

'Put it further in, and put some of the cream

21

on your sex . . . it will slide in more easily, then you'll feel something quite unusual.'

I didn't need any persuading. The almond cream gave me new sensations. This woman constantly anticipated my fantasies. Her buttocks were parted. She pointed her arse at me like a target. I gripped her firmly to bring my erect prick down between her buttocks and into the mouth of her sex. The more I delayed the moment, the more aroused my senses became. Then I made my first approach. The almond cream was warming me up. Migumi gesticulated a little, then arched her body so that she was almost on her knees. Her respiration was intensifying. My prick slowly penetrated and her buttocks closed like two silken veils.

An agreeable warmth spread throughout the lower part of my body and, in that tight zone, my sex gained a new vitality. Migumi guided one of my hands to her breasts and the other to her velvet pussy. She pushed back at me with her bottom, moved from right to left and up and down.

This Japanese girl was an expert, her whole body moved. I had never felt myself to be in such good . . . hands! Her arse was quite different from a Western woman's Her movements revealed an artistry in caressing which I had never dreamed of. She really had got rhythm, a rhythm under the skin, quite naturally. I moved in and out at the same tempo as Migumi. She was laughing and said several sweet things to me in Japanese. I didn't think they needed any translation.

'Try to withdraw your sex a bit and put some more cream on it, that will keep us warm and stimulate us,' she said.

I just kept the tip of the glans inside and put on some more of that fabulous almond cream, of which I did not know the secret properties. It was a tricky business. She told me to be careful to avoid coming out altogether and going soft. But just hearing her voice and the manner in which she was speaking to me kept my sex as hard as could be. So I did what she wanted very precisely.

I massaged her little breasts which were as round as apples. And she pushed her bottom against me with all her strength.

'Come, come, come now! I'll explode with you. Yes! Yes! Yes! I want to feel you spurting inside me . . .'

'You're going to make me yell, Migumi! I hope the neighbours won't hear me!'

'Make as much noise as you like; it will excite me even more!'

I'd sworn to myself that I would make her come before taking my own pleasure. But she must have had more than one trick up her sleeve.

I was not unduly surprised when she said: 'Pick me up by my legs, but stay behind me. I'll keep my balance by putting both hands on the floor . . .'

Carefully and gradually I rose from my knees while keeping my prick between her buttocks. She was light, which facilitated the task. But she had no need of hands. She was at my mercy, suspended from my sex which was buried deeply within her, and, what's more, in a position which I had never encountered before. I was holding the young woman by the hips, and her legs were folded back behind my buttocks.

'Turn me,' she said.

So I did, until the ultimate ascension of sperm into that lovely body. She was surprised by my roar. I was full of exultation, and she gave a deep moan which seemed to be torn from her flesh when she felt me jerk violently, between her buttocks which were wet with almond cream and warm spurts.

I had the impression that I was handling a living doll. A doll which wound itself around me like a rebellious liana, which showed me the paths to follow, the best ways to attain satisfaction. What pleased me in her were her unpredictable impulses, her efforts to find different pleasures, ceremonies which united the subtlest art and fantasy.

We lay side by side. Migumi had thrown her arms back and was looking up at the ceiling. Her extraordinary tranquillity after coming made me search for the calmness which was emanating from her. We remained thus for a little over a quarter of an hour, in complete silence, apart from our breathing, that music of contented lovers.

She got up to go to the bathroom. I could hear water running. She came back to the sitting room almost at once.

'Would you like some coffee or something?'

'I'll have whatever you're having, Migumi.'

'Tea, then.'

'That will be perfect.'

I lit a cigarette. The smoke tasted different that evening. I saw myself in the deserted street again, then the astonishing meeting with Migumi. It seemed to me that I was beginning to enjoy life again; the merest trifle had been all that was necessary, or almost. For a fortnight or so I had been wandering around in the hope of an encounter. The cafés were full of unattractive girls who were more than willing to let someone buy them a drink. I had been striving to find a pearl beyond price in a tacky night-club, but it was chance which had rescued me from my vain nocturnal ramblings. Migumi had opened a new world to me.

The tea was ready. She set down two cups

and went into the bathroom. When she returned, I said with some surprise, 'Isn't your bath full yet?'

'Oh no! It's long. It's quite unusual, a double bath.'

I was astonished. But Migumi seemed to me to be a ripe fruit of many pleasures.

We drank our tea together. I felt like asking her certain questions but restrained my curiosity, preferring to discover gradually secrets that seemed to be in a shadowy zone.

'You were perfect just now. I love your way of sucking and delaying the pleasure. You made me groan from the bottom of my stomach. That doesn't often happen with me. You make love in an oriental way.'

'Maybe. But it is rarely that one finds such a partner. It was you who surprised me the most! I was far from imagining such a wonderful lover. Seeing you in the street, one would never guess . . .'

'Please! Come with me. We're going to take a bath together.'

She took me by the hand and I followed her.

Her bathroom was blue like the southern seas. It was like being in the tropics. Little lamps stood on little tables near an enormous pouf covered with sponge. Her bath was splendid. There was a double bed, mirrors on one wall and a silver-grey ceiling.

White foam covered the surface of the bath water. Before we got in, she took off my kimono.

'You get in first. Is the water warm enough for you?'

'Excellent!'

'Good. Soak yourself, then I'll put some relaxing gel on you.'

Her hands moved over my body with a bracing gentleness. She spread the gel on my buttocks and turned me round to slide her tongue furtively over my sex which had been erect for quite some time. A bathroom is a place eminently suited to excite me. She gave me the bottle and I spread the gel over her body, which was slender and firm, with well-defined curves. I lingered over her breasts, then zestfully attacked her buttocks. Then we both slid down into the water.

We sat facing each other in the bath. She relaxed in the water and I did the same. We teased each other with our feet. She started to massage my sex very slowly, letting me savour the moment, my head resting on the edge of the bath. When she felt that I was stiff and hot, she asked me to take her from behind. She stood up and leaned her hands against the wall, presenting her bottom to me like a ball of rustling foam. My prick was still creamy with the gel she had rubbed on me, so I penetrated her deliciously and effortlessly.

'Don't move!' she said. 'I'll do the moving. Just remain as you are.'

She always had the last word.

Now, she was moving and undulating around my sex which was sliding in and out of her. This position usually sucks all the energy out of me, but the beginning of that evening had been propitious for building up a massive force in me. I was in a state of perpetual excitation and each innovation by Migumi left me wondering what new realm of intense pleasure she was leading me to.

I was in a constant state of erection. Her swaying hips stimulated my sensuality.

She was positively bursting with joy. She exulted with her whole body. I admired her stamina. Migumi's appetite for orgasms was extremely infectious. I melted in her carnal presence. I felt that I was being rejuvenated in that bath where my whole body was in motion. Cares flew away, the only world which existed was a paradise of arse! Migumi was the queen of arse. Her skilful use of it was driving me crazy! I ejaculated, moaning and gasping. I withdrew and clasped her to me, letting my sperm run down between her buttocks. I had slipped my fingers inside her and worked them energetically. We slid down into the water and she started to come.

When we got out of the bath, she dried me, then I put my kimono on. She sent me to wait for her in the sitting room.

It was already midnight by my watch. I had received an extreme and unexpected dose of pleasure. My encounter was going to be an unhoped for education.

Migumi appeared in a flaming red kimono, bigger and thicker than the one she had worn for dinner. She came towards me smoking a cigarette. 'Have you had a pleasant evening?'

'Much more than that! You have relieved me of the fundamental anguish which plagues the casual adventurer: I haven't had to go through all the pointless rituals.'

'I'm pleased to hear you say that. But I shouldn't like you to get a bad impression of me. I wanted to take my pleasure with you because you didn't try to seduce me. It was your kindness and gentlemanly behaviour which excited me. But I should like to ask one thing of you . . .'

'What?'

'After an evening like this I usually want to be alone, to sleep alone. I should prefer it if you were to go home. I'll give you a call tomorrow and if you feel like seeing me again, we can make arrangements.'

'Okay, if that's what you want.'

'Another thing: never call here without

checking with me first. I have a very full schedule . . .'

I took my leave of Migumi. Time had seemed to stand still.

Chapter 2

The next morning I woke up quite late. I had had a good night's sleep, which had put me into a state close to euphoria. Migumi had intrigued me with her programme. But the terms of her contract were very much to my liking. I had the feeling that that young woman had some surprises in store for me.

All that remained in my memory was the frenzy of her desires. She was a sort of de luxe creature, a woman unlike others, who took charge of her fantasies, without worrying what the norms were.

Why should I try to classify, in particular, the type of woman that Migumi was? The evolution of manners and morals seemed to me to be fatuous, a flickering torch held up to try to validate our society where fine words concealed a fundamental prudishness. Who can honestly say he knows the different facets of the modern liberated woman, living in accordance with the impulses of her soul and her physical needs?

From time immemorial there have always been women who have taken charge of their own destinies, whatever the period of history in which they were living. And Migumi was one of those surprising women who could reconcile the most confirmed misogynist with the weaker sex. As for my recent experiences with her, I was anticipating a series of adventures for which I should seek neither justifications nor reasons. With Migumi, I was going to let myself be carried along by the current.

For several weeks I was Migumi's companion, partner, plaything, lover. I lent myself to her desires, I placed myself at her disposal, cancelling all my appointments, postponing all my affairs and staying at home most of the time to wait for her telephone calls. Sometimes I was filled with anguish when she was late in calling. Her work took up a lot of her time during the day. It was difficult to get in touch with her; on certain days, I was forbidden to call her at work. There were reasons for that. Reasons which I came to understand later.

It was not until nearly six o'clock the day after our first meeting that she rang me.

'Would you like to spend the evening with me? I have invited the friend who couldn't come last night. She's very nice.'

'I'll be there. I'll come at about half eight, if that's all right with you.'

'Perfect! See you soon.'

I was filled with an inexplicable excitement. I didn't know whether it was Migumi's tone, or the idea of that third person who was going to be in the apartment that I had left such a short time previously.

I took a bath, then dressed myself elegantly and perfumed myself with Signorici. To kill time, I watched the news on the television.

I rang Migumi's doorbell. She was radiant, her smile galvanised me. She accompanied me to the sitting room, where I saw her friend.

'This is Misako. She works in my agency.'

Migumi left us to get acquainted with each other. Misako was dressed extremely fashionably: a tight-fitting black dress by Alaia, and strange-looking pumps which seemed to be painted on, in which I sensed the mark of the designer Tokio Kumagai. Her hair was slightly curly and her face radiant with youth. She couldn't have been more than twenty-five.

Misako served me with an aperitif while Migumi was preparing dinner. She had told us to start without her, which we did.

Misako told me about her fashion parades at Paris, London, Berlin and New York. She represented several Japanese and French designers and a new Cambodian couturier. It was a new experience for her, and her engagement-book was becoming fuller and fuller. When she questioned me about my activities, I replied evasively, letting her understand that I worked in the music trade, records. She seemed interested and mentioned numerous artists whom she admired, notably certain black singers. She knew quite a bit about them. She told me about certain video clips which had impressed her. She recorded them on TV and often played them.

During this conversation, Migumi was busy in the kitchen. Misako got up to lay the table. I saw Migumi give her some cards which looked very much like menus. She put one on each plate.

Misako came over and seated herself on the divan again with a sly air which left me feeling perplexed.

She noticed and looked me straight in the eyes. 'The menu is very special, this evening. Migumi has an incredible gift for making her parties special. But you already know a bit about that, I think. Anyway, I don't think you'll be disappointed.'

'I like women who astonish me! That's so rare these days.'

Migumi invited us to sit at the table. She placed me at an equal distance from Misako and herself.

'I have prepared these little cards specially for us three. It's a way of getting acquainted. Please, read the text.'

So I familiarised myself with this highly unusual menu. The text was divided into several paragraphs:

1. In Migumi's house, the chosen guest's sole aim must be to seek sexual pleasure. Each of the partners must submit themselves to the eventuality of increasing that pleasure either by means of the imagination, or by another person's invitation.

2. The extra guest – in this case, Misako – must receive satisfaction as well as the instigator of the game. The hostess may ask to withdraw with one of the partners.

3. The games and ceremonies must be shared between the partners. Each of the partners' fantasies must be acted out. The male guest must submit to the demands of the feminine partners.

4. Away from this place of pleasure, the associates are free to lead their lives as they please. Each meeting will be fixed by the mistress of the house.

5. Everyone is free to use accessories to increase pleasure.

6. In the house of pleasure, the partners must obey the rules of propriety, of courtesy

and of their respective cultures. No dangerous practices will be tolerated. Sexual intercourse will not be one-sided; all partners are equal and will share each initiative.

7. Every sexual practice is a social act, one of the elements which form our culture. The partners should exchange knowledge and open new ways of attaining pleasure for each other.

It is understood that the seven clauses of this code agreed between the partners here present, this evening, should be carried out humorously, frankly and voluptuously.

When I had finished reading, Migumi and Misako looked at me enquiringly. The programme was agreeable to me. I didn't hesitate to inform them of my enthusiasm immediately.

Migumi poured me a glass of burgundy to celebrate our agreement and said, 'My dear friend, you are not obliged to make a decision immediately. Think it over. After dinner you are free to consider something else . . .'

'Not at all! I'm your guest, and I want to get to know you better, Migumi, and you, Misako.'

So that was settled, and then we applied ourselves to the business of eating the excellent meal which Migumi had prepared. I no longer tried to understand what was happening to me. I was floating around in another world. A world governed by two delightful Japanese girls. Migumi, a mistress woman, and Misako: a piquant girl-flower!

When we had finished, Migumi asked Misako to start our evening as she had done with me the previous day. Misako got up and went over to put a record on. She chose sensual music. I heard the opening bars of 'Sexual Healing' by Marvin Gaye. She came back to the table and poured herself a small glass of sake which she swallowed at one go.

Migumi winked at me and began to speak in Japanese. I didn't know whether she was addressing me or Misako. The latter had already slipped under the table and I could feel her hands unfastening my trousers and delicately extracting my sex, which was already standing up. She put her hand on it, massaged it, rubbed it, manipulated it between her finger and thumb, then ran her tongue which was heated by the sake over it.

I said not a word.

Migumi took my hand and placed it on one of her breasts, which thrust up under her blouse of beige silk. I pressed them, going from one to the other. I played with the dark points which were becoming firmer and firmer. She closed her eyes and savoured my caresses. At the same time, under the table, Misako was producing almost unbearable sensations in me.

I had changed my position so that she could take me entirely into her mouth. She was drinking my whole sex! She had one hand under my buttocks. Migumi opened her mouth to tell me it was divine and that Misako excited her in that position.

I felt like masturbating Migumi and fucking Misako. But for the moment, Misako was sucking me furiously deep in her throat. I felt the semen building up in my testicles and Migumi was moaning softly. Then I gave a slight cry, trying hard to restrain myself.

Migumi opened her eyes and said, 'Are you going to come?'

'Soon,' I replied.

She said sharply to Misako, 'Go gently, wait for me!'

I did not understand straight away. But my second cry was the starting signal for what she had foreseen. I could no longer hold on and my sperm spurted into Misako's mouth. And suddenly, Migumi got under the table as fast as she could to get at my frothing sex. One mouth left me and another one started to suck me. My stomach started to rumble. Those two Japanese girls were literally sending me to heaven and they continually surprised me, at every moment.

I felt strange in that position, bent right over the table, my legs folded under the chair. They were gripping my sex which was in the last throes of excitation. My two Japanese dolls were laughing heartily under the table.

'Ah! Ah! Ah! Not a drop more . . .'

'That's putting it mildly, you're great at sucking, no one could resist such artistry!'

'It's what we like best!'

They had worked together to bring me off. And I burst into frank and sonorous laughter.

They emerged from under the table and each drank a glass of sake. Misako asked me whether she had come up to my expectations. I acquiesced volubly.

Migumi proposed that we should go into the sitting room. She disappeared into the kitchen to make tea and coffee.

Misako sat down beside me on the sofa. I drew her to me and started to feel her breasts. She made no effort to resist and helped me unfasten her dress. I uncovered lovely smooth shoulders and started to suck her breasts, which were somewhat bigger than Migumi's. They were warm and an intoxicating perfume was coming from them. She let it happen, preferring me to take the lead. Then I put my hand under her buttocks and insinuated it as far as her slightly damp sex. Imagine my surprise when I discovered that she had no hair there! It was completely smooth. Her skin was soft.

She murmured in my ear, 'Do you like it like that?'

'Yes,' I said. 'It's very exciting.'

'When I'm shaved, caresses have a double effect on me. I like to feel a mouth moving around the whole area which surrounds my sex. You'll find it even more exciting. It's such a lovely feeling.'

'I'd like to fuck you with my tongue!' I said eagerly.

'Come on then.'

She raised her dress, took off her suspender-belt and lay down on the sofa. Then I started to lick that naked pubis, moistening the slender lips, which were as well-defined as the fringes of a living oyster, and retracting at each caress from my vibrant tongue. She was making me terribly excited.

I was gradually pushing my tongue further and further inside her. I pulled her lips open, tickled her, here and there, then suddenly took possession of her clitoris. She gripped my head with her hands. I had found the sensitive spot. I redoubled my lingual caresses, fastening my mouth to her naked sex which hung slack and open. Suddenly she pushed me away.

'Not so fast, I won't be able to keep up later on.'

'But I want to make you come.'

'Okay, but not too much . . .'

I went back between her legs like an explorer anxious to discover new territories. I licked her lips with the tip of my tongue so as not to precipitate matters. But that only made me even more excited. I felt as big as an orange. Misako put her hand in my trousers and pressed my cock. She was beginning to moan when we heard Migumi returning with a tray.

'So, you couldn't wait for me! I can't turn my back for five minutes. Do you find Misako so charming, my friend? Or is it her bare sex which turns you on?'

'Both,' I smiled.

'That's understandable. But I want to do things my way,' said Migumi.

'You're right, I was forgetting our agreement.'

'I only said it because this is a three-way party. We haven't finished yet, and Misako is often more demanding than me. I'm just giving you a gentle warning, Patrick.'

'I realise that. But if I myself want to do certain things, are you willing to go along with them?'

'But of course! That's part of the agreement,' Migumi and Misako exclaimed in unison, as usual.

I sensed that they really were accomplices. Yet when Migumi had seen me setting about Misako on the sofa, she had seemed somewhat ruffled. Was it because I felt less at her mercy and was showing it too clearly? Or was it perhaps because I found Misako as seductive as her? In fact, Migumi had acted as she did in order to signify that it was she who had conceived this ceremony and the agreement. Misako was her plaything as much as myself. But what kinds of playthings were we for Migumi? She had class, elegant manners, a sophisticated way of receiving guests and a subtle use of words. She had once more become the woman I had encountered in the street twenty-four hours previously: charming, polite, absolutely independent and with an organising ability that was brilliant.

'Misako, would you like to put on those musical videos which you like so much?'

Misako got up, hunted through the video-rack and set the recorder going. We were finishing our coffee. I saw the first images of the black singer, Prince, appear. Dressed in a transparent raincoat, he was emerging from a cloud of smoke and advancing, holding a microphone and moving his hips with an extraordinary sensuality. He started his famous song, 'Automatic Lover'. Two girls who formed the chorus were behind him, swaying to the rhythm of that lascivious funky music which was all the rage with American and

European teenagers. The words of the song got straight to the point:

'You ask me if I love you, it's
automatic
A.U.T.OMATIC, just tell me what to do.'

The tone was very expressive. And the girls moved in a very hot way.

'See what happens at the end,' Misako said. 'I've recorded different songs, as you'll see, but this is my favourite, together with "Delirious" and "Lady Cab Driver".'

Migumi was dancing to the rhythm of the music and Misako had lowered the lights. She pushed the table back too, leaving a wide space between the screen and the two sofas. I didn't understand the point of all that. Migumi disappeared for a few moments, then came back wearing her red kimono and carrying two others, a green one for Misako and a canary one for me. She asked me to change quickly. Misako did so in the middle of the room, moving like Prince's girls with absolutely choreographed gestures. As for me, I knew nothing of the art of undressing like that but I carefully observed all of Misako's most sensual movements.

The images succeeded each other, and at the end of the song, just as Misako had said, the two girls approached Prince, then led him to another scene.

A big bed was there. They undressed him. All he was wearing then was a pair of black underpants, gloves of the same colour and his boots. The music continued, red and blue smoke swirled around the stage. Now the singer was tied to the bed, one arm at each side, and the two white girls began to caress him then, suddenly, they were holding whips.

I could hear him moaning, and they gave him a few lascivious, gentle strokes, in time with the music, without really hurting him.

Misako turned towards me, an enquiring expression on her face. She wanted to know whether I had understood the scene. I smiled at her, but I didn't know whether she wanted to whip me. Certainly not. Then she came towards me with Migumi.

'We're going to play the video in the bedroom. Misako and I would like you just to let things happen. We're taking charge of you. The music will help you. You can keep your kimono on for the moment, while we prepare the bedroom, and the rest.'

I didn't dare ask her any questions about what they intended to do. Not for a moment did I think that they intended to whip me. Then I remembered the contract, one clause especially: 'No dangerous practices will be tolerated.'

That was inscribed in article six of our agreement which had been presented like a menu at the beginning of the evening.

I suddenly felt much more eager to find out what new ceremony my two Japanese ladies had devised!

Migumi invited me to join them in the bedroom.

She had turned on some neon lighting whose red, blue and yellow colours conferred a particular atmosphere upon that spacious room. Screens made of mirrors were placed on each side of the bed and I saw that the ceiling was made of some reflecting material which gave the impression of a gigantic mirror.

Misako took me by the hand and installed me on the bed. From the pocket of her kimono she produced two cotton thongs and tied my hands to the top of the bed. The video-films continued their performance while all this was going on. As for Migumi, she was preparing an assortment of drinks on a trolley which she brought over to the bed. Then that young lady made me spread my legs and gave me a mischievous smile.

'It will be easier for us if you spread your legs. Anyway, I'm going to tie them to the foot of the bed. It will increase your pleasure and your concentration!'

I agreed.

Now Misako together with Migumi was imitating the movements of Prince's girls and swaying her hips. They both came closer to me. I already had a hard-on under my pants and my prick wanted to get loose. Migumi licked my neck and chest. I tried to kiss her but she moved away quickly, leaving me helplessly salivating. Misako was gradually moving her head nearer and nearer to my sex but did not take it into her mouth. Her tongue caressed delightfully, and she placed her thick, juicy lips on it. Feeling the contact of that soft skin on mine made me even harder. That woman certainly knew how to raise the sap of joy. She got on to the bed and pulled my pants down, revealing my hard, erect sex, which seemed to be looking for somewhere to go.

Migumi began to laugh and took her kimono off. I discovered that her breasts were caught in a brassiere which encircled rather than supported them, and she was wearing a pair of black lacy knickers which left her cunt and her ass free.

Misako had started to lick my glans with a very wet tongue. My body contracted, I raised myself up slightly in order to look at her small breasts which were above me. I wanted to take them violently into my mouth.

While this was going on, Migumi was making her first delicate advances to me. She leaped quickly on to the bed and sat astride my chest, her sex close to my face.

'Will you suck my breasts first?' she said.

'That's what I've been waiting for, Migumi. It's almost torture being a victim, a trembling victim!'

I took each of her breasts into my mouth in turn. In fact, my position permitted me enough movement to satisfy her desires. At that moment, Misako pulled my pants further down and started to suck me properly. I was in heaven. Her creamy tongue whirled round my sex like a propeller. And Migumi pressed her breasts against my face, then rubbed herself against my chest.

Misako untied my feet and took my pants right off. She took possession of my hot balls, massaging them skilfully. One of her hands went under my buttocks, the other stroked me with studied slowness.

'Is that nice?' Misako enquired.

'Oh yes! I want to fuck you.'

'Not yet, give me a little more time. Anyway, we must wait for Migumi. Migumi, are you ready?'

'Soon,' she replied.

Misako guided my prick to her smooth sex and used the glans to separate the lips. She breathed a 'Yes!' which was a signal for Migumi, who had moved so that I could suck her. I had hardly put my tongue into that juicy cunt when I felt a formidable pressure! Misako had just sat on my sex, making it penetrate her with a fantastic thrust of her buttocks. It was hot and velvety. She started to rise and fall carefully to avoid losing me. And the more I sucked Migumi, the more excited I became.

Misako was moving from left to right, making my cock explore every corner of her. I really could feel her engulfing me. Her manner of using her sex was disconcerting! That continual coming and going sent shivers along my spine, made all my limbs jerk spasmodically. I took Migumi's clitoris between my teeth and nibbled it in the way she liked. She began to moan. Misako gave little cries from time to time. I thrust my buttocks up suddenly, penetrating even deeper. I heard her say several words in Japanese and Migumi answered.

'We'll come together . . .'

'Oh yes, Migumi! Misako!' I said.

Misako was driving me beyond my powers of endurance. The way that young woman moved her buttocks was killing me! I decided to give as good as I was getting. Migumi was moaning continuously now and Misako increased speed frenetically in order to match the rhythm of the music we could hear.

Migumi uttered a long, muffled cry. I continued to lick, feeling that she was coming, and Misako gave a great gasp as I discharged, jiggling about all over the place. My whole body lost itself in them. They possessed me completely.

Migumi rested her head on my chest and Misako slid between my legs, continuing to caress my moist sex, which was still very warm.

They untied my hands, and I was able to put them round my two lascivious dolls. They each took one of my legs between their thighs and we savoured those moments of calm after the storm.

Migumi got up and served us with a cocktail which she had prepared with sake and other ingredients: ginger, rounds of kiwi fruit and lemon.

The drink reinvigorated me. We watched the rest of the videos.

Misako brought in a bowl which contained a fragrant cream. Migumi was lying on the bed and turned over on to her stomach. Misako rubbed some of the cream between her friend's buttocks and then handed me the pot. I rubbed some between her buttocks and pushed my finger right in, drawing a hum of passing pleasure from her.

'What are we going to do now?' I asked.

'We're going to play a game, if you want to. But you have the right to ask us both for a favour.'

'But what is the game?'

'You Frenchmen like to do it dog-fashion, don't you? Well, you've got to do it to us, both at the same time, giving each of us equal attention, and the first one to come has to pay you a forfeit.'

'Whatever I ask?'

'Whatever you desire. But nothing dangerous.'

'And suppose I make you both come at the same time?'

'It's possible . . . You'd have two forfeits, but it would be a difficult thing to do.'

They were absolutely right. But it was not my intention to make them come at the same time. I wanted Misako to come first. Her way of moving her vagina had made me come more strongly than I had ever done with any European woman. I wanted her doubly, for her youth and the beauty of her body excited me to the depths of my being. As for Migumi, that was another matter. She had the air of a great lady whom one desires on certain occasions. But Migumi's arse had certainly wrung some wonderful sensations from me the previous night.

I caressed them again. They got themselves

into position. I ran my hands over their upraised bottoms, tapping their buttocks and rubbing their pussies.

I took my prick and slid it into Misako first. I penetrated slowly at first, then suddenly pushed all the way in. She gave a cry.

'Are you all right?'

'Yes, I was just surprised. You were so quick!'

'Well, it's got to be like that because of the game, and I'm not going to keep Migumi hanging around either.'

Migumi was nicely opened up and it was like sliding into velvet.

The game consisted in doing it faster and faster so that their excitement had no chance to wane. And I gave my two geishas my prick in time with 'Delirious', which Prince was murmuring on the video, accompanying our frantic movements.

In this double-arsed position, my hard-on was becoming stiffer and stiffer. They teased me, asking me if I was going to be able to hold on until at least one of them came. But the game consisted in making them both come, even if one came first. I took another cocktail from the trolley by the side of the bed and drank it to keep my strength up.

Migumi pushed vigorously with her arse whilst Misako wiggled hers tenderly when I penetrated it. The rhythm accelerated. I went from one to the other.I caressed their breasts and from time to time parted their buttocks in order to stimulate them more. It was obvious that Misako was about to melt with pleasure. That threatened to set me going too, but on no account must I ejaculate before their orgasm. So I started to apply more pressure to Misako. I buried myself to the hilt, then withdrew slowly in order to increase the pleasure. Migumi was continuously uttering little cries of pleasure, which were as penetrating as the voices we could hear on the video.

After a few more energetic strokes, Misako came first with a long harsh cry which covered the voice of Migumi, who had started to move faster. I gave Misako one last thrust and she collapsed on the bed. I slipped my fingers into her pussy while Migumi now had my prick all to herself. I pushed as hard as I could. Migumi begged me to wait for her, which I did before entering into a violent back and forth motion which brought us off together.

We'd come together. It was wonderful! Misako caressed my buttocks while I was still on top of Migumi.

She ran her fingers over my buttocks and probed me eagerly. Migumi began to caress Misako's breasts. I disengaged myself so that Misako could rub my cock as seemed to be her wish. She did it so well that I became stiff again. I didn't know whether it was the cocktail or the cream which was having that effect on me. The girls seemed to be delighted. They began to laugh, and I murmured some soft, expressive and sexually exciting words to them to revive their energy.

'We must get our strength back. Don't forget that Misako owes you a forfeit,' said Migumi tenderly.

I hadn't forgotten and I certainly intended to claim it. They disappeared into the bathroom for a few moments and came back wearing kimonos. I had installed myself on the bed and was watching the videos. I had an idea concerning Misako, who I wanted to possess on her own.

In Migumi's bedroom there was an exercise-bar for dancing. That was it! Migumi brought in some little almond balls and offered me another cocktail. I asked Misako if she was ready to satisfy my desire. She said that she was.

'Misako, you see this bar, I want you to stand facing it and put one leg up on it. I'll take you like that from behind. It won't be too difficult for you, will it?'

'Not at all! I do a lot of dancing and gymnastics.'

She posed gracefully and I followed her.

55

That position excited me terribly, I had at last found the place and the person for that superb acrobatic feat!

I pressed my body close to hers from behind, caressing her between her thighs, feeling the perfect line of her legs and the opening of her shaven pussy. True delight! She stroked me a little and I started to penetrate her, holding her by the hips. A real ballet figure!

I pushed up into her. The openness of that position was wonderful. The air passing between her sex and mine produced electrical sensations, a kind of variation of hot and cold which maintained my erection to the maximum.

'Hum! That's super,' she said.

'It's marvellous, but not always possible, but with a girl like you, Misako, talented, versatile, it's out of this world!'

Migumi turned up the volume of the music, and winked at me. I blew her a rapid kiss. She approached us and saw that Misako was receiving intense pleasure in that position. She caressed her friend's breasts then asked if she could intervene between us.

Misako shook her head and asked Migumi to wait her turn as agreed. Misako was approaching orgasm and I was moving in and out with increasing rapidity. She was very wet indeed. As for Migumi, she lightly stroked my buttocks several times, which greatly increased my pleasure. And Misako was bent double and moaning like a lost soul when I spurted my hot juices.

She withdrew from the bar and went to lie down on the bed, taking me with her. I licked her breasts again, whose points were swollen with the juices of her pleasure, points which seemed like Chinese cherries. I nibbled them tirelessly, drawing a last long moan from her.

Migumi asked me to stop then. I looked her straight in the eyes, questioningly. I understood that she desired me.

'It's late. I think Misako is tired. Aren't you tired?'

'I'm in top form, thanks to your drinks and your cream, Migumi,' I replied.

'That's not surprising, they're aphrodisiacs imported from Japan. But I'd like to go to bed now. I have a heavy work schedule tomorrow morning. If you don't mind, my dear friend.'

I acquiesced, got dressed and had one last drink. Misako did the same, giving me a smile of complicity. I was at their disposal, and, all the time, their smiles kept me in suspense. My little Nipponese knew how to dispel any tendency to ill-humour on my part.

Misako left first, as ordered by Migumi. Then Migumi told me not to seek to contact Misako apart from the meetings arranged by herself. I didn't protest. I observed the rules which I had accepted at our first meeting.

Again she requested me to leave. I did so, kissing her hand.

When I arrived in the hall downstairs, I heard her voice on the intercom.

'Hello, are you there?'

'Yes, Migumi.'

'I'll be here tomorrow afternoon, I'll give you a buzz, wait for me to call you and don't try to ring me! Sleep tight.'

'Okay, and I hope you sleep well too.'

Chapter
3

The next day, Migumi's cocktails continued to have some strange effects on my whole body. My head was afflicted with intense itching and inexplicable sensations of coldness. I wasn't suffering from migraine, but it seemed to me that my entire body was still in a voluptuous lair, a hot cocoon, surrounded by invisible women.

I took a quick shower and drank several cups of very hot coffee.

I remembered Migumi's instructions but they didn't really suit me at all. I was dead keen on seeing Misako again. But how to go about it?

At about eleven, I decided to go to the Rue La Boétie where Migumi's fashion agency was. I found the building and took up my position in a café which faced it on the other side of the street. And I waited for the lunch hour.

At about one, Migumi appeared, surrounded by four Japanese men. I saw her give a card to each of them. I felt perplexed. Then she led them towards a restaurant which was on the same side of the street. She let them go in but didn't follow them. She retraced her steps and disappeared into the building from which she had come. A few minutes later, she reappeared with Misako. They were speaking volubly, then Migumi pointed to her watch.

I saw them from my café, where I had been for more than an hour now.

Suddenly, they separated. Misako went down the Rue La Boétie towards the Faubourg St-Honoré while Migumi took the Rue Pierre-Charron towards the Champs-Elysées. I waited in the café for a few minutes, then I left hurriedly, trying to catch Misako up, while at the same time making sure that Migumi had gone.

Misako was walking slowly, so it was easy to catch her up.

I called her name. Misako turned and regarded me with a rather embarrassed smile. 'What a surprise! Is this a chance meeting?'

'Not really. I wanted to see you without Migumi, so . . .'

She wouldn't let me continue. 'You know that's not possible. Migumi explained it to you. And then we might be seen . . .' She looked all around.

'She went off in the other direction. I don't understand what there is between you. Migumi didn't really tell me anything about her relationship with you! Nor the rest . . .'

'It would take too long to explain.'

'Yesterday evening, it was perfect with you. Couldn't we meet this afternoon about six?'

'No. I've got some appointments, but give me your telephone number. I can't promise anything at the moment. Migumi must know nothing about it. Okay?'

'Good. This is intriguing and exciting too. Here you are!'

She took my card which had my number on it and made off rapidly, not forgetting to smile at me. How unpredictable those Nipponese girls were!

I returned home at six, passing by the place where Migumi lived. I wanted to ring but hesitated to do so. Then, plucking up my courage, I rang the bell. No response. I rang again, waited for a few more seconds then heard a voice.

'Who is it?'

'It's Patrick . . . I was just passing and . . .'

'I told you I'd be busy. I've got a business meeting. I'll give you a call later. Goodbye.'

She cut the connection before I had time to reply. I wondered what was going on in her

63

apartment. I went back to my own place which was at the end of the street.

There were several messages on my answering-machine, but nothing from Misako. I tidied up a bit and put some music on.

The telephone rang. I rushed to answer it. It was a former girlfriend who was after me and was wondering why I hadn't replied to her letters. I did my best to calm her down, promising to get in touch soon. I looked at my watch and saw that it was already a quarter to six. I cut the conversation short, saying that I was expecting an important telephone call. My former girlfriend insulted me, calling me all the names under the sun. I was obliged to hang up on her.

I was overwhelmed by a strange sense of excitement. I wondered what was going to happen that evening. Would it be Migumi or Misako who would ring first?

A strange feeling took possession of me, a feeling which I had never before experienced, of being tossed about between two women, between two mysteries. For a time, these sensual and aimless ruminations calmed me down.

But I was pacing about the room like a bear in a cage when the sound of the telephone ringing broke into my thoughts.

'Hello!'

It was Misako.

'Sorry about this afternoon, but I wasn't free. Migumi asked me to do something, and it was impossible for me to refuse, you do understand?'

'Well . . . no! But I accept that your work must take up a lot of your time.'

'That's true, I had to go to a hotel to act as a guide for an important visitor from Tokyo. It took a bit more time than I'd reckoned on, then I had to go and see Migumi to tell her about it.'

'I rang her doorbell this afternoon. I disturbed her.'

'I know. I was there. We were discussing business matters. Why don't you stick to the agreement? You're too curious, my friend!' She said that with a laugh. 'We have a lot of work to do at the agency, and sometimes we have to receive guests in our homes. Migumi makes all the arrangements.'

'Look, Misako, I'm not very clear about how you conduct your business. Would you like to come here this evening?'

'I'd be delighted to, all the more so as what we did yesterday excited me a great deal! But I'm expecting a call. I'll ring back later. Okay?'

'Is it a call from Migumi that you're expecting?'

'Yes,' she replied, with great frankness.

'Anyway, she's supposed to give you a ring too, isn't she?'

'True. But that will make no difference to our arrangements for this evening.'

'I believe you. Bye for now.'

She hung up and I looked at my watch: it was already seven o'clock. I became absorbed in abstruse and incongruous thoughts about Migumi and Misako. I poured myself a Martini with a dash of gin and settled down to wait for a call from either Migumi or Misako. I wondered where this three-way game would lead me.

I became absorbed in conjectures, for numerous questions came into my mind when I thought about what Misako had said. Exactly what role did Migumi play in the agency and what place did Misako occupy?

What was beginning to get to me was the possibility of having to spend the evening on my own. My first night with Migumi had been surprising. My second night with Migumi and Misako had surpassed my intentions! I just couldn't accept the idea that my two Japanese girls, who were so willing and so enterprising, were going to leave me in the lurch so soon. That didn't seem to me to be in keeping with the ceremony which Migumi had invited me to participate in. Then there was the famous contract we had entered into the second night.

The telephone rang. I looked at my watch, it

was eight o'clock. It was Migumi. She apologised for the delay and suggested that the three of us should meet at her place at about ten, if her meeting finished in time. She would let me know if it would be possible at exactly five to ten. She hung up before I had a chance to ask any questions.

In that decisive tone of voice it was easy to recognize her true nature which was that of a woman of action. Migumi ordered her life in a precise and calculated fashion.

At that moment, I could only see one solution. It wasn't long before Misako rang again.

'Hello, I'm sorry, but I can't come yet, it will have to be later.'

'What's going on, Misako? I've got the feeling that your playing hide-and-seek with me. I want you terribly!'

'Me too. Give me another couple of hours, then I'll be with you. Listen for my call at about ten or five past. Don't ask any questions, I'll be on time . . .'

'It's terrible, all this playing around!' I said, without much conviction.

'A Japanese proverb says, "To each according to his tastes; certain insects like stinging nettles."'

'Well, that's appropriate. What can I say?'

'It'll be worth waiting for, I promise. If you're patient, you will be able to help me to do a gymnastic exercise of which you possess the secret! So, when I arrive, you must obey me as soon as I enter!'

After these words, she hung up.

Her promises caused a sudden surge of excitement in me. My prick stood up. I thought about her naked sex, her smooth skin, her cherry nipples and the way her vagina swallowed me.

These images tortured me for two hours.

I put the radio on. A fairly explosive funky tune was playing. 'That was "Animal Instinct", by the Commodores,' said the disc-jockey. Ten o'clock already. And not a word from Migumi.

The next five minutes seemed to me to be interminable. Each second was like Chinese torture. I'd walked several kilometres in my apartment when the ringing of the telephone put an end to the marathon.

'Hello! Is that you Misako?'

'Yes. How impatient you sound! I'll be there in a few minutes. Are you ready?'

'I am yours to command.'

'See to it that the lighting is as soft as possible, then we'll see how well you serve me.'

There the communication ended.

I followed her instructions immediately, subduing the lighting as much as possible and switching on my answering-machine so that we shouldn't be disturbed. I put a bit of soul music on, knowing she liked that.

She arrived quickly and rang the doorbell. I heard her voice on the intercom.

'Leave your door open, go and sit on a chair and make sure you're blindfolded.'

I did what she'd told me to do. I could hear her approaching: she must be wearing boots, to judge from the noise she was making. Then there was the sound of the door being closed gently.

I was aware of her coming over to me. The music was creating warm rhythms. The atmosphere acquired a strange density. Undoubtedly, she was close to me for I could hear her breathing, could smell her perfume and hear the rustle of clothing. Installed there on a chair, my eyes blindfolded, I waited for a few more moments. Then she took my head in her hands and pressed my face hard against her stomach, then against her smooth pubis.

'You must remain blindfolded until I come. You must say nothing, just suck me. I want your tongue deep in my pussy, my lips sucked, my thighs bitten. I want your saliva on my lips and your face wet with my juices.'

She had said all that in a ceremonial tone of voice but extremely softly. She stood between my legs and I felt her buttocks with my hands.

That evening Misako smelled of orange-blossom and a heady essence which tickled my nostrils and filled me with sensations close to a state of intoxication.

She was naked under her coat.

My tongue penetrated her deeply, then I started to run it up and down. I became even more excited. I was wearing a dressing-gown and could feel my own sex throbbing.

She began to speak to me again. 'You disobeyed, today! Ah, yes, go on, keep on like that . . . your tongue feels marvellous . . . make it stiff like a prick!'

While she was speaking, I went on with my caresses. She gave me the impression that I was taking part in a religious ritual. Misako guided my head, then put one of her legs over my shoulder and held me in that manner. The position became as pleasant for her as for me. I went further down, to the beginning of her taught, round little buttocks.

'Yes, don't stop, go right into my furrow, I love that . . . You've only just started! Our contract with Migumi has not really been broken, you've just taken one partner. But that will be all right.'

When she spoke of Migumi, images of the preceding night's frolics flashed into my mind. I wanted to squeeze her body, eat her breasts, fuck her violently. But I was fucking her with my tongue. I rubbed my nose against her clito-

ris. She contracted several times as I teased
that moist little fruit. Then I took it between
my teeth and she felt better.

'You're doing fine . . . In fact, I think you're
going to make me take off. Ah! Ah! Ah!'

She laughed and rubbed her sex rhythmically against my face. She was getting wetter
and wetter. She went on talking more and
more loudly. And I continued to suck her
deeper and deeper.

Her pussy was constantly moving around but
my mouth never let up for an instant. I wanted
to get up and rub my sex against hers, but that
was not allowed. She held me in place between
her leg and her hand. That wet sex had become
my whole horizon now. I kneaded her buttocks
and gradually pulled them further apart as I
continued to suck greedily. Her clitoris dissol-
ved between my teeth and she started to come
with long, progressively louder cries, alternat-
ing with calmer moments, then resuming her
orgasmic chanting which made me so stiff that
it hurt. I was lightly slapping her buttocks
faster and faster. Then I pulled them right open
in order to let some air into her wet crack and
enlarge the opening of the wrinkled raspberry
which was gradually opening up anyway under
the pressure of my forefinger.

She was in a state of jubilation. She said 'Ah!
Yes, I forgive you for everything . . . Hit my

71

buttocks again. Oh yes! Like that . . . Migumi won't know a thing about it.'

I increased the pace and she came well and truly, bringing her foot back down to the floor. I strove to hold her in place and pressed my face hard against her once again, thrusting my tongue deep into that sopping pussy. She sank to the carpet and fell forward over my knees. I could feel two erect nipples pressing against me and, without giving me any time to react, she drew out my cock and took it into her mouth, sucking greedily like a starving woman.

I had been waiting for that moment for what seemed an eternity.

She took my sex right in. Her tongue was very active. She sucked the glans then let it go for a brief moment. After that she rubbed me with two fingers and sucked energetically at the same time.

Suddenly she passed her hands under my buttocks and took my prick right into her mouth which was moving ceaselessly and keeping perfect time with the music I had put on. I was in a state of exultation! I felt my hot sperm, so long contained, rising. Misako took it in her mouth and swallowed every last drop. I was twisting about on the chair, quite unable to contain myself. I gave a loud cry and fell down on to the carpet.

She came and removed the blindfold from

my eyes. And she asked me to remain silent. Which I did, after having uttered that final cry of pleasure. The lovely girl caressed me again and I cupped and moulded her breasts. Her coat half covered me, while my dressing gown had come right open during our loving struggle.

'Now it's your turn to call the tune,' she said.

She got up and asked where the bathroom was. I showed her and asked her to wear the kimono which I had put there.

I too got up and turned the music down. I prepared some drinks for us and thought about what I'd like to do with Misako. In fact, there were two things I'd like to do. But would she agree? The scene we had just acted out had made a profound impression on me. The memory of the afternoon and the constantly postponed meetings kept coming into my mind.

So I opted for the first of my desires. When she returned, I offered her a drink, while looking deeply into her eyes.

'Would you be willing to do . . . two things for me?'

'It depends what they are.'

'Nothing unreasonable. Promise that you'll do what I ask?'

'Very well.'

Her docility excited me. With a bit of luck, I

was going to find out a secret. I let her refresh herself, finished my Martini and said, 'Misako, what I am going to ask you will surprise you. I just want to know exactly what there is between Migumi and you and what goes on in that agency. Why do you have all those mysterious meetings?'

She was completely taken aback by my words. Her expression changed abruptly.

'That was the last thing I was expecting! I think you've gone too far. My work is my business and my private life is quite separate. Our contract with Migumi is a secret which you share, but it's quite separate from our social life, isn't it?' she said forcefully, as if to convince me.

'No doubt. But you agreed to do as I asked! You've nothing to fear with me. And anyway, Migumi would have told me sooner or later.'

'This is terribly embarrassing. I would have preferred to talk to Migumi about it first. But perhaps it's too late, now.'

Misako helped herself to another drink. I sensed that she was on guard now.

This is what she told me that night, the second of our acquaintance.

'When I met Migumi for the first time I was seventeen. I wanted to make my way in the world and was especially interested in the world of fashion, and the possibility of becoming a mannequin. So off I went to Tokyo with a little case and my savings. When I arrived in the big city, I felt a bit disorientated. I had just one address, that of a distant cousin, and nothing else.

'So I spent my time visiting all the agencies and fashion houses. I received quite a number of rebuffs and you can imagine how I felt! After a few days of trailing round the agencies, I presented myself at one whose address I'd discovered in a fashionable magazine which praised its originality, its youthfulness. This agency was something of a pioneer for it employed numerous young designers and their clothes were exported all over the world. The mannequins followed the collections into certain great European and American salons. With such a reputation, the agency demanded very high standards. At that time, I dressed in the Western style and had the appearance of a real Parisian.

'So I applied to this agency. I was interviewed. They gave me some clothes to try on, they made me move around while some men and women asked me questions about my family. I answered briefly. One of the men became impatient. I heard him say, "What is she doing?" I didn't know who he was speaking to. Then they asked me questions about my private life: what were my ambitions as regards the profession and many other things that a girl as young as I was could have had no knowledge of at that time. I was afraid when one of them said, "There's no point!" Then nothing. A door opened, just a few seconds after those words were spoken, and Migumi appeared. She impressed me immediately. And her colleagues seemed satisfied. They entered into consultation.

'I was seized with panic when the voices grew louder. Migumi looked me straight in the eyes and asked me to get undressed. I didn't understand that she wanted me to strip in front of that gathering of people. So I started to walk towards the exit, at the same time taking off my jacket, when Migumi addressed me for the second time: "Take your clothes off here."

'There was no time to think about it, so I did what she said. I had had enough of running round the agencies. Migumi inspected my body and asked me various questions: "Do you like travelling? Meeting people? Big social gatherings? Would you like to work with me and travel around with me?" When the questions stopped, I was overcome by a sudden attack of nerves and blurted out a loud "yes" and fought to hold back a flood of tears which was threatening to overwhelm me. Then I broke down, and with my last gasp asked if I'd got the job. Migumi came over to me, took me in her arms

76

and whispered "yes" into my ear. The others had gone. She gave me back my clothes which were scattered on the floor.

'I became calm again and someone showed me Migumi's office, where she was waiting for me. It was near the end of the day. I'd found a job. Then Migumi invited me to dinner and to move in with her in order to complete my education. There was a strong possibility of my becoming the agency's top model. Gradually, I came to realise that the agency needed to develop. Migumi had worked out a lot of ways for bringing about this development, concerning the extension of the business to other countries. One of these ways consisted of using the agency's most beautiful women as call-girls for powerful businessmen.

'Migumi assured me of her protection, gave me everything I needed, taught me how to conduct myself in the world. I had nothing to lose. I had left my family. I didn't have a lover. And I wanted to travel. So I followed Migumi everywhere she went and participated in her most personal initiatives.'

She finished her story with a gleam of laughter in her eyes. 'Now you know everything. As for the contract which Migumi has produced, it's the first time that has happened. Anyway, it surprised me when she told me about your meeting and the arrangements she wanted to make. In fact, you've been lucky with her, and with me!'

'It's all happened so fast and so unexpectedly. The pleasure that women like you give is so rare. I still can't get over it, Misako. And don't forget that you promised me we should go on for a long time tonight!'

'Why else am I here? You've been too long without exercise. I'm just as capable as Migumi of taking initiative. She's a bit snowed under with work at the agency, at present.'

'What would happen if she found out about our meeting?'

'Don't worry. Migumi has set up a sort of haven of peace between you and me. This fantasy enables her to forget business worries for a while. Migumi knows how to season everyday life with a bit of excitement!'

'But what if she questions me?'

'Impossible! I'm the only one she's likely to question. Although I'm still dependent on Migumi, I've a schedule which leaves me with quite a lot of free time. Anyway, you could at least offer me a drink. Have you got any sake?'

'Yes, I bought some after my evening with Migumi, but I've also got some champagne.'

'Champagne! Have you got something to celebrate?'

'Most definitely. But are you going to be my

guide this evening and lead me to a Fujiyama of unknown pleasures?'

'That depends on whether we have champagne or sake.'

'Let's go for the champagne then!'

'It's going to be terrible for you!'

'Why?'

'Is it chilled?'

'Yes, but why do you ask?'

'Don't ask questions. Just leave everything to me.'

'I'm in your hands. Even here in my own home.'

'What does it matter where we are? We should drink it in the kitchen.'

'The kitchen?'

'Yes, because it seems that that's the place where the French most often make love.'

'Where did you get that from?'

'Don't you ever read the statistics they publish in magazines?'

'Look, let's drink it in the bedroom.'

'Okay! But on one condition. We'll do it in accordance with a ritual whose delights I have experienced. But first, let's have a glass of sake, neat.'

A smile played upon her gracious features and I filled two glasses. We drank together. She finished hers before me and slipped to her knees, pulling my dressing-gown open. She took hold of my prick, breathing warmly upon it, then put it into her mouth, which was burning hot from the sake, and gave me something like a sudden electric shock. She withdrew quickly, as though she had just wanted to give me a foretaste of pleasures to come, and dragged me into the bedroom, not forgetting the bottle of champagne.

The lovely girl took off my dressing-gown at top speed then made me lie on the bed. I had no idea what she intended to do. She blindfolded me, then once again caressed my erect sex.

Suddenly, I heard the cork pop from the bottle of champagne, accompanied by her joyful laughter. Then she ordered me not to move or cry out.

She moved closer to me, then I felt a sensation of coldness. She was slowly pouring champagne on to my body and drinking it as it settled on me. She sucked me with an incredible expertise everywhere the champagne went. The sensation of coldness disappeared with those caresses, to be replaced by a quite different feeling. I experienced a kind of short-circuit: I gave a violent start, then relaxed and enjoyed that hyper-voluptuous sucking.

She gently poured champagne all around my sex and started to lap up every drop. The game consisted in not making the bed wet and she was covering the whole surface of my skin with her frenetic mouth. The pleasurable sensations intensified as the champagne reached the sensitive parts of my body. She poured some champagne directly on to my sex and drank the lot. The slurping sounds coming from her mouth doubled my excitement. When I moved a bit too much for her liking, she pulled me up short. Then I felt her tongue lapping up the drops which were running down my balls and even wandering between my buttocks. The sensations were almost unbearable. I was fast approaching my climax. She continued to suck me implacably. And when she heard me groaning, she poured some more champagne on my sex and quickly drank down the hot–cold cocktail of fizzy sperm.

She swallowed every drop. Then she lay down on top of me, vigorously rubbing her body against mine in order to communicate her heat to me.

After a few calm moments, Misako ordered me to do the same thing to her, telling me not to spill one drop of champagne on the bed and to cover her whole body as rapidly as possible.

To begin with, she rolled over on to her stomach and parted her thighs. Little by little, I spilt champagne on to her spine and then lapped up every last drop. She hardly seemed to be affected by the coldness. Then the perverse creature asked me to pour champagne between her buttocks and lick it out. She raised her bottom slightly, and I poured some into the cleft. It was a perilous moment for me. Then I thrust my tongue between those dainty hillocks and lapped up everything that was there.

She turned over and I started to encircle her breasts with my champagne kisses. I poured more and more and eventually reached her naked, quivering sex. The liquid ran down her slit and I drank it all while she started to suck me again. We came at the same time in a moment of exemplary euphoria! Our senses were so inflamed that the orgasms seemed to be torn from us. Our bodies writhed to the rhythm of our greedy, eager sucking.

The sake and the champagne were taking effect. I felt as if I were in a sort of soft cushion, my head was whirling as a result of Misako's impenitent caresses.

I sank into a state of semi-consciousness, but was dimly aware of a noise. A far-off sound of water came to me. I didn't know whether it was a glass being filled or a shower running.

I saw a form moving vaguely as if it were behind clouds. Misako appeared to me one last time. The memory of her kissing me ran through my body. I quivered. Then nothing more.

Chapter
4

When I recovered consciousness, it was still dark. I felt for a body next to mine, but didn't find one. I raised my head and looked. A light was still on in the sitting room. I tried to get up and found that I was sweating. I looked at my watch which indicated four o'clock in the morning and wondered how long it was since I'd dozed off, and when Misako had left.

I went into the bathroom, intending to put my head under the cold-water tap. These words were written in lipstick on the mirror: 'See you tomorrow perhaps, Misako.'

Then I went into the kitchen to get some aspirin. I returned to the sitting room and noticed that my answering-machine had recorded a message. Had that happened before my session with Misako or during my sleep?

I played the message, and heard Migumi's voice: 'Sorry about tonight. I'd like to introduce you to someone tomorrow. I'll be in touch later to make definite arrangements. Goodnight.'

Migumi's voice woke me up suddenly. Her message left me feeling perplexed. I thought about Misako and our contract. I felt a sudden, strange sense of excitement which disappeared as quickly as it had come. I went back to bed and thought about my new life with those Japanese ladies, while I waited for sleep to overtake me. Lustful images kept coming obsessively into my mind. So obsessive were they, in fact, that I ended up in a state of total exhaustion with all those intertwined bodies moving around me, touching my skin, absorbing me completely, sucking me everywhere.

The morning passed very quickly. I finally got up at about three in the afternoon. For several days now I had completely neglected my own affairs and my friends. I shut myself up for practically the whole day and waited for the evening to come with a kind of jubilant impatience. Sometimes, I would go for a walk in my own district, towards the end of the day, then return to await Migumi's orders concerning our meetings.

At about six-thirty Migumi rang. Her voice seemed to be vibrant with good humour. She told me what the menu would be that evening. I was to go to her apartment to dine.

I wore a dinner-jacket as requested.

When I arrived at her place, she opened the door and accompanied me to the lounge where a young Japanese girl was sitting. She stood up and greeted me in the traditional way by bowing her head. Migumi introduced her as Akiko, her little cousin. Migumi said a few words to her in Japanese and she left us and disappeared into the kitchen.

I asked Migumi if Misako would be joining us.

'Are you missing her already?' she said maliciously.

I didn't know what to say and hid my embarrassment with a smile.

'Misako's already here. This evening she will serve us with Akiko's help.'

I was surprised, but something must be behind that.

Suddenly, Misako and Akiko emerged from the kitchen together, carrying trays of drinks. Misako nodded to me discreetly. She was wearing a kimono. Akiko served me a glass of sake while Misako attended to Migumi.

Akiko slipped down beside me on the sofa while Misako sat down near Migumi.

Migumi presided over the little gathering and she clinked her glass against mine, saying,

'Here's to the health of our contract! I've included my little cousin in our ceremony. She's entirely at your disposal and you can ask her to do whatever you like. But I have a small favour to ask of you tonight.'

'Thank you, Migumi, but what is this favour?'

While we were talking, the youthful Akiko had got down between my legs and was unfastening my zipper.

'You know something about the work I do in the agency. I have to deal with people passing through, our foreign distributors. One of our clients, who has three shops in the United States, is here. Usually, I take her out somewhere or organise one of the rather special evenings she likes. I couldn't offer her the model in question as he's away from Paris for a couple of days. She's due here at about ten and I'm asking you to escort her. You won't regret it because she's charming.'

'You're giving me a token, Migumi?'

'No, rather a way of consolidating our contract and sharing our secret. Isn't that right, Misako?'

Misako acquiesced without batting an eyelid.

I was beginning to understand the way our meetings worked. Pretty little Akiko was giving me an energetic blow-job and making it impossible for me to think clearly with the expert way in which she was using her fingers, tongue and mouth. Migumi and Misako smiled at me mischievously. They looked at Akiko, who was sucking me delightfully. Migumi was finishing her drink while Misako very lightly caressed her friend's breasts.

The feel of the sake on my penis was once again giving me wonderful sensations.

Migumi and Misako left the room so that I could be alone with my little climbing-flower Akiko. I took her on to my legs and made her sit down on my sex. She balanced herself on me and started to move up and down in a leisurely way which made my whole being vibrate. Her sex was tight but it gradually opened to my pressure. Soon I was all the way in. She started to move faster then did an abrupt about-face which left me breathless with amazement. She did a pirouette, and I found myself staring at her back and my sex had stayed in her all the time. I placed my hands on her hips and took charge of the rhythm myself. It was a very enjoyable position. My stalk penetrated her and she squeezed it with skilful contractions. I jerked her up and down above me, she moved from left to right and her little ass drew long shudders of delight from me. She was getting wetter and wetter and my rigid stalk drew titil-lating lapping noises from her as I shot my sperm into her. In the paroxysm of our orgasms, the girl sat down completely on me and squeezed my spurting sex in a last contraction.

After this session with Migumi's new recruit, Misako brought in the dinner which consisted of various *sushi* and raw fish.

Migumi questioned me about Akiko. I replied that she was already quite an expert for a girl of seventeen. Akiko changed her clothes and came back wearing a leather miniskirt and a red silk blouse.

Migumi filled me in on the American woman who was to join us later. Then she informed me that she had told her that I was one of her colleagues. I was supposed to deal with publicity and catalogues presenting the agency's collections.

During the course of the conversation, I noticed that Misako remained silent, occupying herself exclusively with serving Migumi and myself. I didn't dare to make any allusion to our intimate encounter of the previous night. But it seemed to me that Migumi was aware of our secret.

To be honest, that didn't worry me. I was quivering with excitement at the idea of meeting the American woman and spending another evening filled with surprises, arranged by Migumi.

The apartment was steeped in an atmosphere of warmth and cordiality. And Migumi teased me from time to time.

Someone rang the doorbell. Migumi went to the intercom. It was the American woman.

She opened the door and a woman of about forty entered. She was wearing a wolf's-skin coat which she unfastened to reveal a skirt slit on four sides. Her eyes were of the same limpid grey as the Baltic Sea in mid-winter. When we shook hands, I noticed that her hair had red tints in it. She didn't seem to be wearing a brassiere under her blouse; the points of her breasts were clearly revealed.

Migumi chatted about this and that, then served us with one of those special cocktails of which she possessed the secret.

'Drink that and tell me what you think of it!'

'Is this one of your famous mixtures, Migumi?' said Kathleen, the superb American, in a sensual tone of voice.

Migumi nodded in assent and gave me a wink which comforted me. Misako had found her smile again, and the little cousin, Akiko, had disappeared into Migumi's bedroom. As for Kathleen, she was very voluble.

'Migumi, I'm sure that you've put some oriental aphrodisiac in this!'

Migumi made a dainty gesture with her

fingers signifying that she had only put a dash in.

I broke my self-imposed silence and said, 'Oh, it's only an aphro-dizzy-act, Kathleen!'

They laughed while I got up and went to fetch my coat. The glasses were empty. After the cocktails were finished, I had to do as Migumi had directed me.

I invited Kathleen to come with me. We left Migumi and Misako.

In the street, we walked to Kathleen's car, a black Chrysler automatic with dark windows. She suggested that I should drive and take her for a tour of the ring-road. The idea seemed a bit ridiculous to me.

I raised no objections, however, and off we went. She asked how long I'd been working with Migumi and what I did exactly. I replied that in my spare time I sometimes wrote articles about fashions and new foreign designers.

We talked a bit more, then she put a jazz tape on. I recognized a Cole Porter number, 'I Get a Kick out of You', sung by Billie Holiday. Very appropriate!

When we reached the ring-road, she asked me to go a bit faster. She pulled her split skirt aside.

'Are you a good driver?' she demanded.

'Yes. Don't worry.'

'Oh, I'm not afraid, but it might get a bit complicated for you.'

I couldn't see what she was getting at. Then she placed her hand on my thigh and guided my hand to hers. She unzipped me quickly and gripped my sex hard between her fingers. She asked me to keep my eyes on the road and to continue to drive at a moderate speed. Which I did.

The American woman fished out my sex and rubbed it diligently. My hand was exploring between her thighs. She cuddled up closer to me and when she could feel that I was nice and hard, bent over and started to suck me with little jerks of her head. I watched the road with even more concentration. What was happening was exciting me very much. She pulled my trousers down a bit more so that she could take me right into her mouth. It was an extremely dangerous thing to do. I was caressing her too and she was bobbing up and down like a crazy woman. My pleasure was all the stronger because the speed at which we were moving was filling me with excitement. And the more she sucked me, the more I tended to accelerate. She became aware of the speed and sat up in order to calm me down.

'I adore it this way in the car but do be careful. The more I suck you, the more you

93

want to step on it. I'll give you a breather before you come. Don't do it without warning me first! Okay?'

'Okay, Kathleen. But it's torture, even though it's wonderful.'

'I think you're wonderful. I'll give you a surprise soon. Ah, how lovely it is like this!'

We almost did the grand tour of the ring-road, with me fighting to restrain my orgasm and going faster and faster. What an exploit! She was giving me head more and more energetically when I warned her that I was about to come.

She quickly withdrew her mouth from my prick and made me take up an oblique position on the seat. The Chrysler was spacious, which allowed us considerable freedom of movement. She continued to rub me and removed her skirt in a flash. She wasn't wearing panties.

What happened next filled me with very real fear.

Kathleen ordered me to watch where we were going and on no account to take my eyes off the road. The next thing that crazy lady did really filled me with panic.

She sat astride me, facing the windscreen, and leaving me just enough space to see the road. She reassured me, saying that she was used to doing it, and introduced my sex into her

– it had been kept hard by these new sensations. Then my reckless companion began to
move up and down, supporting herself with her
hands on either side of the seat. I was overwhelmed by her incredible behaviour! We
covered a few more kilometres, then she asked
me to drive towards the Porte d'Auteuil. Whatever happened, she wanted to come as we left
the ring-road behind, in unison with my orgasm.
It wasn't easy for me to restrain myself but that
new position gave me fresh strength and I
made a few thrusts which Kathleen appreci-
ated. With my free hand, I was kneading her
superb breasts. She was absolutely marvellous.
She'd turned the music up. And I kept
accelerating without getting out of breath. We
reached the peak of our excitement as we were
whizzing along towards the Boulevard Suchet.

The time I spent in that car seemed to me to
be infinite!

She zipped my trousers up and put her skirt
on.

'Migumi said you wouldn't disappoint me!'

'Well, I wasn't expecting anything like this.
You're a dangerous lady.'

'Not really! I'm impulsive and I like strong
sensations.'

She made me laugh several times. I tried to
get her to tell me what she had in mind for me
next. She was unwilling to let on before we

arrived at the apartment which had been placed at her disposal during her stay in Paris. I respected her wishes.

She made me stop in front of a building in the Boulevard Suchet. I parked the car and we got out.

Her apartment was on the third floor. She opened the door and helped me off with my coat. She invited me to install myself in the sitting room. I took note of the perfectly realised reproduction Louis XV ceiling, the Persian and Chinese carpets and the Japanese dolls in little glass-fronted cupboards. Numerous big mirrors hung on the walls of that immense room. There were four leather sofas and some armchairs covered with thick turquoise silk.

She returned with two glasses and a bottle of champagne in a bucket of ice. She'd changed and was wearing a black silk dressing-gown, and around her neck was a string of pearls. That lovely woman looked at me with shining grey eyes. We drank a toast to our new-born relationship and I wondered what the rest of the night would bring.

She turned the television on but cut the sound: a film was showing. I watched her moving around the room, stopping now and then to rearrange various objects, then she put some music on and asked me to dance. Afterwards, we had some more champagne and finished the bottle.

I tried to get to know Kathleen better, but she answered my questions evasively. I learned that she had been married and that her divorce had caused a scandal in Beverly Hills, where she lived. Her husband had found out about her innumerable nocturnal jaunts and her sexual eccentricities.

She invited me to go into the bathroom to change.

A kimono was there at my disposal. Then I waited for her to summon me.

'You'll find me in the bedroom in a few moments. I'll tell you when it's all right to come in.'

I waited for a few minutes in the corridor which was going to lead me to an energetic encounter with Kathleen. I could still feel those breasts which I'd squeezed in the car. I was impatient to explore her body and to feel it against mine. Kathleen had long slender legs and moved like a film star: the very image of the hypersensual, hypervoluptuous woman of action!

She called to me in English in a lascivious tone of voice.

When I entered the bedroom, a bedside lamp was spilling a soft violet light. Pearl-grey walls gave off a gentle and pleasing luminosity.

Kathleen was reposing on the bed quite naked, on her stomach. When she became aware of my presence, she asked me to turn on a tape-recorder which was on a low table.

'It's a cassette which I got in New York. It's something new that couples use to add a little spice to their evenings. This one is special: it gives you a whole series of relaxing massages. I want you to follow it. There's some cream for you to use on the table.'

So I set the cassette going. Then I heard some background music and the voice of the woman who was presenting the programme. I took the pot of cream, which smelt of musk and other perfumes, and spread it on my hands.

The programme began. I sat astride Kathleen and followed the instructions which were given quite slowly.

First of all, my hands slid down her long neck and on to her shoulders. Her skin quivered at my touch. I felt myself to be the master of the situation. She was between my thighs with me suspended over her. Her arms were stretched out to each side of the bed. Her breasts were flattened in that position and one could see their edges protruding from under her chest. I went round them with my hands, following the instructions.

Then the girl on the cassette said that the

woman should spread cream on the man's sexual parts. Kathleen turned round, took the cream and carefully put some on my sex, which stood up between her agile fingers, and on to my taut scrotum. Then she turned round and I carried on. I massaged her buttocks from the bottom to the top. That must have produced some pleasurable sensations, for Kathleen quivered under the pressure of my hands. After this preparation, her buttocks began to jiggle, they began to open up a bit. The second phase consisted of sliding my prick along her well-lubricated crack, in accordance with the logical progression of the cassette. That massage between those plump white buttocks made my glans go red and swell to bursting point: it was looking for a home to go to. For Kathleen's part, she was pushing but the way seemed to be blocked. I was coming and going in time with her. She cried, 'Push, push!' And I pushed for all I was worth.

Suddenly, she turned round violently and pulled her legs right back. Then she asked me to put them on my shoulders. She guided my hands to her breasts, which I squeezed and massaged.

She took my prick and massaged it with long, cool fingers. I was now in a kneeling position and she presented her sex to me, her hairy pussy which was rubbing itself against my scrotum. She made a swift movement and my hard cock entered her. I penetrated her little by little and brought her legs into position around my torso. Kathleen's buttocks pressed against my belly as I went right in. We were still following the cassette when the music became louder. Kathleen indicated to me that the moment had come to accomplish the act.

She wriggled around my sex and pushed back at me more and more. She was half hanging from my body and kicked her legs out behind my back. She was giving superb cries which were turning me on with greater and greater intensity.

'Harder, go in deeper, go on . . . Ah! yes, step on it like you did in the car! Rub my breasts! Crush them! Pull them . . . Yes, like that!'

'Ah, Kathleen, you've got a cunt which bites, which is too hot for words! You're a right slut! A great fuck! I've got a load to give you!'

'Yes! Oh, Go on . . .'

She was moving about all over the place. It was difficult to prevent my sex slipping out. Her pussy was as wet as could be. Then I started to jerk in and out rapidly, moving from left to right. After that I pretended to withdraw my sex and suddenly pushed it right back into her vagina. She exploded with a painful wailing sound and went rigid, tightening the grip of her thighs round me. My sperm flowed and I cried out stridently as it spurted. She relaxed and I slipped down on to her body which stretched out under me with nervous, spasmodic movements.

'Ah! It's a long time since I had such a good fuck! I came everywhere, mon amour! Your cock has done me a lot of good.'

'You've got an extremely voluptuous nature, Kathleen. Your whole body is perfectly attuned to your sex, it's marvellous!'

I nibbled the tips of her breasts. She drew me closer and put my prick between those firm, heavy globes. She rubbed me tirelessly and groaned as she did so. She was wringing every last drop of pleasure from me. My prick had become super-stiff again. I felt that it would stay like that for hours.

Kathleen began to flick me with her tongue, then started to suck me. She was enjoying herself like some cheap floozy. But I was unable to ejaculate. My prick was hard and hurting me. I wondered if it was Migumi's cocktail which was producing that effect.

Kathleen asked if I was insensible to her caresses. I said that that was not so.

'This always happens when I've come too much. I have a permanent hard-on.'

'That's great! We'll take a shower together. I'll get it down for you!' she said maliciously.

We went into the bathroom, and she ordered me to rub her with a sponge under the shower. Then it was her turn to rub me. She passed her hand under my buttocks and once again took hold of my cock. I fingered her gently and sucked those lovely breasts.

She leaned forward, supporting herself by gripping the wash-basin, and made me stand behind her. I aimed myself at that inviting ass. We were still wet and creamy. She spread her legs and bent forward even more, offering me her hot entrance which was wet and slippery from our love-making. Then I penetrated that tight opening, which gradually yielded as my sex went in.

'Are you well in?'

'Yes, it's all right.'

'Don't move for a while. I've got a surprise for you!'

Her buttocks enveloped my balls. I was right inside her. Then she squeezed and got a good grip on my sex. She shifted her legs slightly, then began to move backwards and forwards. A comforting warmth spread from my sex to my abdomen. I gripped her hips and started to push too. My prick was firmly established inside her. It was she who was directing the operation. The pressure of that beautiful ass squeezed me hard. She was pushing back at me like a madwoman. She crossed her legs again. She made me quake deliciously and frenetically. My sex felt more comfortable and I could feel my excitement mounting. She tickled me, which made me laugh happily. She gave me a few more seconds and promised me that I was going to explode inside her. I caressed her pussy as she squeezed my cock between her ample buttocks. My breathing accelerated as I came, shooting hot sperm into the warm depths of her body. She relaxed, letting me come and go in the final shuddering pleasure. I beat against her in the violence of that pleasure. She took my hands and placed them on her breasts. I covered her with my body, feeling the lines of her bones, every particle of skin. I kissed the warm neck and smooth shoulders and pressed my lips to her back and her superbly rounded hips.

We drank some more champagne on the bed. She told me how satisfied she was with our evening. She hadn't expected to find a partner who would take part in such mad pranks, especially the one on the ring-roads. I was no less satisfied.

Kathleen made it clear that she had complete confidence in Migumi. That was why she had been willing to try me. Migumi had left her in no doubt that she could ask anything of me.

I suppressed a desire to laugh. Kathleen's presence in that room and her manners made a deep impression on me. I told her of the unusual pleasure which I had experienced in the car and then on the bed, listening to the tape. Then I asked if she could get some for me. She replied that Migumi had a complete set. I was surprised, but perhaps Migumi was reserving them for a later occasion.

We were still almost naked, drinking some more champagne. I didn't know whether we had emptied a third bottle. We were sitting facing each other in an armchair near the bed, light-heartedly discussing the many positions for making love. She told me that she felt more pleasure with men she had met by chance or who had been introduced to her by reliable friends. She always liked to be in charge, but liked the men to show some degree of originality. Kathleen had learnt about these new ways of enjoying herself at the parties which Migumi had organised for her benefit during her numerous visits to Paris. She had also taught the American woman certain oriental techniques, Chinese and Japanese: to know how to delay pleasure, to conserve one's strength and that of one's partner, to change positions when excitement was mounting too rapidly.

As she was speaking, my organ became erect again and protruded from my kimono. She saw it and slipped down to take it in her mouth. She was on her knees, sucking me again. She withdrew her mouth in order to tell me to ejaculate all over her face when I felt my sperm rising, to let it run over her tongue, her lips, everywhere. Those words were like a detonator to me. She pressed warm fingers to the root of my sex to make the sap rise as quickly as possible, ran her tongue along the whole length, then took me right into her mouth.

I warned Kathleen that I was about to come. I raised myself up enough to have her face opposite my sex. She withdrew so that only the tip of her outstretched tongue was touching it and the liquid began to flow on to it and on to her lips. She continued to stroke me and the last jet sprayed all over that pretty face. The perverse woman licked her lips and lapped up every drop. She polished my knob with her tongue and pressed out the last drops of juice. The greedy woman drained me completely!

I was beginning to realise how much she loved sucking. I wanted to take her once more but didn't have time to say a word because she climbed on top of me, using that lovely ass to push my stalk into her big open pussy. She moved magnificently and sought her pleasure by turning around in every direction. She gave a long moan of satisfaction and collapsed on to me. I sucked her breasts again. They felt hot. We came together with all the strength that remained to us.

I dressed while Kathleen was in the bathroom.

I waited in the sitting room for a few moments, then she arrived.

'I have to leave very early tomorrow morning,' she said. 'Would you like me to ring for a taxi? It's been a lovely evening.'

'Yes, it has. I hope we can meet again the next time you're here.'

'It's possible. That depends on Migumi and a number of things.'

She telephoned. I could tell from her manner that she was intensely aware of other people's desires, their thoughts, and knew just how to put them at ease. Kathleen left me her card, which gave the addresses of her shops in California and New York.

The taxi arrived a quarter of an hour later.

As I was about to leave, she took an envelope from her handbag.

'This is for you. Migumi asked me to give it to you before you left.'

I left, putting the letter in to my pocket.

The taxi was waiting for me. Kathleen

appeared at a window and waved me goodbye. I replied by bowing to her in the Japanese fashion. I saw her smile, standing there on the balcony, then I got into the taxi and told the driver where to take me.

Chapter
5

When I arrived in the Rue Tiquetonne, I still hadn't opened Migumi's letter. I was still under the spell of Kathleen and her magnificent body. As the taxi carried me home, I recalled the dangerous start to the evening on the ring-road. A feeling of being an egg wrapped in cotton wool took possession of me.

I paid the driver and went into the house. I took the keys to the apartment out of my pocket together with Migumi's letter. The effects of fatigue and alcohol were beginning to make themselves felt, but my impatience to read the letter proved to be stronger.

My Dear Pat,

Considering your recent experiences with me, I do not think you will have disappointed Kathleen. She probably gave you a few somewhat frightening moments, which you undoubtedly coped with with your commonsense and savoir-faire. To make up for the two evenings spent away from the house of pleasure, you are invited to attend a friendly gathering which will be held in a certain manor-house tomorrow evening. Please wear formal evening-attire.

Sleep well and have a nice day tomorrow.

Be here at seven-thirty precisely. *Sayonara.*

Migumi.

I fell asleep a few moments later after having read the letter.

I woke up and had breakfast at about midday. I was surprised at the way the days were slipping by without my realising it. But I paid avid attention to the nights which Migumi organised with her characteristic precision. It seemed to me that my space-time continuum had been turned completely topsy-turvy. The days were insipid without the presence of my two Japanese girls.

I was quivering with anticipation when evening came. I began to prepare myself for my night out at about five in the afternoon. I had some tea, read a few pages of a good book and listened to some music. Images of last night with Kathleen came into my mind again.

I remembered the cassette she had played in the bedroom, Migumi's cocktail which we had drunk together.

I decided to take a bath and shave and did so quickly in front of the mirror, taking care not to cut myself.

I went into the bedroom to put on a shirt, a bow-tie, my shoes, and to press my dinner-jacket which was a bit the worse for wear as a result of the previous night. I dressed quickly, for it was already six o'clock.

I went back into the sitting room to listen to a bit of jazz. I put on a record of songs from the great days of the Cotton Club and enhanced the pleasure by sipping a Martini.

The sound of the telephone ringing interrupted my reading.

Migumi's voice had the same effect on me as a gust of wind re-animating a dying fire. She invited me to join her earlier than she'd said. I glanced at my watch, it indicated seven o'clock.

I arrived at her place five minutes later. She opened the door and I saw that she was wearing a marvellous black silk dress which was agreeably low-cut. A pearl necklace around her slender neck enhanced her lovely smooth skin.

'I asked you to come earlier for reasons relating to our contract. You haven't forgotten about it?' she said.

'Definitely not.'

'I'm in the habit of keeping a written record of all my ceremonies like the old Chinese court ladies, the *nu-che*. That's what they were called. They copied down the programme of sexual ceremonies in red ink. I'm telling you this because I wasn't present when you were having fun with Kathleen. That slight breach of our contract was an accident.'

She stopped speaking, for Misako had just come in carrying a tray with tea on it. Misako was resplendent in a fiery red dress, which was also of silk, and which ended above her knees. Her presence excited me terribly. I greeted the young woman and she responded with her customary smile.

Migumi spoke: 'Thank you, Misako. I haven't got time this evening to note down everything you must have to tell Misako and myself. Misako, will you fetch the recorder?'

Misako got up and brought over a little walkman which was perched on the stereo-equipment. She inserted a cassette and set the recording mechanism in motion.

Migumi gave me a cup of tea and asked Misako to note down certain details on a writing-pad.

'Go on then, please, Kathleen must have made quite an impression on you with "The Nanny-Goat in Front of the Tree . . ."'

114

Migumi surprised me. 'What is this "Nanny-Goat in Front of the Tree" then?'

'It's the name given to a position in the sex-manuals of ancient China and Japan. You've still got a lot to learn. Kathleen loves to do it in a car!'

Obviously I remembered the position in question. So I told Migumi and Misako all about my evening with Kathleen. And they wanted to know everything in detail. I did my best to oblige them, and my two Japanese ladies seemed satisfied.

We were ready to go to the party. Migumi invited us to take our places in an old Austin and set off in the direction of the quais towards Bercy, then joined the Eastern autoroute. I really had no idea where we were going. Then Migumi explained that the manor-house we were visiting was situated on the banks of the Marne, more precisely at La Varenne-St-Hilaire. Migumi spoke warmly about the site.

'It's a bit of countryside close to Paris. There are some very lovely houses and two or three excellent restaurants recommended by Gault and Lillau. At one time, many artists lived there. Anyway, I'm sure you're familiar with the famous French films which were made there, in the studios at Joinville.'

'Of course. *La Belle Equipe, Mon Oncle* and

Le Diable au Corps, by the young writer Raymond Radiguet who lived in the region, didn't he?'

'That's right. Do you recall that scene in *Hôtel du Nord* when Arletty says to Louis Jouvet on the bridge: "Atmosphere, atmosphere . . . Go your lonely way to La Varenne, good fishing!" And here we are in fact . . . this is La Varenne.'

We were driving along the banks of the Marne as Migumi finished speaking about that fantastic period. But I didn't know yet whether the fishing would be good in that manor house. Migumi had just mentioned a fashion-parade which was to take place there, but nothing more.

She parked the car in a little street which overlooked the quay, and where there was a big building surrounded by tall trees.

It was a very old manor, certainly, built at the end of the nineteenth century.

Migumi rang and someone responded in Japanese. She gave her name and the door opened. We climbed several steps which led us to the great oak door of the manor itself.

A Japanese in formal dress admitted us. Migumi conversed volubly with him and inspected the entrance-hall, where vases of flowers were set out. She indicated to him that one of them was placed badly. He rectified the

116

position of the vase. Then he opened a second door, which led into a great hall.

About twenty Japanese women were present in that room which must have been more than a hundred and fifty square metres in size. The decoration was modest and in a simple modern style. There were several black and grey leather sofas, some armchairs of the kind popular in the fifties and sixties but re-fashioned to suit modern taste, and little halogen lamps which cast their light upon the different angles of the room. At the back of the hall there was a long table, on which was laid out a buffet supper for the convenience of the guests.

Migumi walked across to the assembled women. We followed her. She exchanged greetings a trifle nervously, introduced me and enquired about the arrangements for the evening. A woman pointed to the floor above and Migumi appeared to be satisfied. I had no idea what all that meant.

As my intimacy with Migumi gradually grew deeper, she seemed more and more to be mystery incarnate, a living mystery. A pure gift. Her movements, her way of behaving gave me an intense impression of a sensuality which was constantly animated and communicative.

Suddenly, Migumi's voice broke into my meandering thoughts.

'The guests will soon be arriving. I have to receive them. Sit down here with Misako. I'll introduce you to some of my friends later on.'

'Don't worry, take your time. I'm anxious for us to get to cruising-speed!' I replied.

'Oh, my goodness! They're here. The parade will be beginning in a few minutes.'

Migumi left us and we sat down on one of the sofas. A charming Japanese girl served us with cocktails.

Misako had recovered her good humour and spoke to me about the party, which was being given to celebrate the agency's anniversary. She told me that the Japanese managing director would be there that evening and that Migumi would certainly introduce me to her.

Within a few minutes, the great hall was filled with people, mostly Japanese. Only a few Westerners were present.

The parade began with music which put an end to all conversation.

The mannequins descended the two staircases which framed the room. A woman came forward and read out a few words in Japanese. She must have been giving the names of the designers and the styles which were being presented. The mannequins moved around gracefully and often seemed to be almost dancing in time with the music.

People had begun to unbend somewhat by

the time the parade had finished. Soon every-one was crowding round the buffet. Migumi came over to us accompanied by a man and a woman.

'I'd like you to meet Madame Kei Ko and Mr Akira, our London agent.'

I greeted the beautiful Japanese lady whose glance electrified me. She addressed a few words to me in English. Migumi praised the quality of my fashion articles. That was the cover she had given me. The man spoke a few words to me in French. I told him how delight-ful the parade had been. He was extremely pleased.

Misako fetched drinks for all of us. Then Migumi drew Madame Kei to one side and spoke to her in Japanese. I saw her smile. Then they rejoined us. Kei Ko drank a toast with me and with the others.

'To what is to come, certainly. I should like to have a few words with you a bit later on,' she said in English.

I nodded my head in agreement. And she went off to join some other guests who were waiting for her. Akira followed the lady. I remained with Migumi and Misako.

The lighting was being gradually dimmed. Couples formed for dancing. I had a few more drinks.

Migumi drew my attention to the fact that

certain women wore brooches pinned to their dresses.

'You see them, Pat? Well, they're available. If you feel in the mood for it, they're the ones you should approach! They really do know all about the art of love and they'll give you the most exquisite pleasure.'

'Is that what you promised me?'

'It's only a part of it! The night is young and you mustn't be surprised by whatever you might see, here and there.' She winked at me and left me to finish my drink. 'I'll leave you for a while,' she said.

She disappeared among the guests, followed by Misako.

The alcohol was beginning to take effect. I needed to visit the toilets. A waiter told me they were upstairs.

When I returned, I noticed that some of the men were being sucked off on the sofas. Others were suckling at breasts which had been pulled out of corsages. This was obviously going to be a very colourful party. And the sight of those couplings excited me terribly. I looked for Migumi and Misako but couldn't see them.

I was going to go to the buffet for another drink when I found Madame Kei Ko by my side. She took me by the arm and invited me to dance. I followed her into the crowd of tightly entwined couples.

We spoke about various things, then she whispered in my ear, 'Migumi has told me that you're quite brilliant when it comes to making love. I know all about the episode in the car with our American friend, Kathleen!'

I didn't know what to say. I pulled her a bit closer. I could feel her small round belly pressing against mine. She made me quiver with excitement. I felt myself growing stiff and pressed against her sex. She gave a little sigh of pleasure. I murmured a few words in French which she didn't understand.

I had a terrible hard-on. Pressing against her like that, I was almost indecent: I caressed her buttocks furtively.

She drew away and said, 'Not here. If you want to, I've got a room on the second floor. Go and have a drink, and come up in five minutes. The door of my room is blue, at the top of the stairs. I'll be waiting for you.'

My heart beat faster, I shouldered my way to the drinks and asked the girl who was serving for a sake cocktail. She prepared it for me and I drank it straight down.

I was anxious to get to know Kei Ko better.

The five minutes passed quite quickly and I went upstairs. On the first floor, buyers were flicking through catalogues outside a series of rooms which I assumed must contain the clothes which the mannequins had presented at the beginning of this extremely pleasant evening. I wormed my way through the little crowd and climbed to the second floor.

When I arrived there, the corridor seemed very quiet. The blue door was there as Kei Ko had said, right at the end. So I knocked and heard her inviting me to enter.

When I went in, I saw the room glowing with red light. A ray of white light filtered from a half-open door to one side, which was undoubtedly a bathroom.

'Get undressed,' Kei Ko called, from the bathroom.

In a few seconds I was naked and waiting to participate in the ceremony which this woman, of whom I knew nothing, might perhaps have in store for me. I was going from surprise to surprise, from pussy to pussy.

She appeared wearing a suspender-belt and high-heeled shoes, with her breasts jutting from an extremely tight half-cup brassiere.

I moved towards that erotic vision, my stalk erect. She took a few steps towards me and knelt in front of my sex which she took in her hands and started to play with. She began to lick it, running her tongue along the entire length of my member which was trying to enter her mouth. Then she caught hold of my

122

buttocks and took my stalk right into her mouth and withdrew it as slowly as she had taken it in. She went on sucking in the same leisurely way, her head moving slowly backwards and forwards. She was salivating copiously and the wet tongue wrapped itself lovingly around me, sometimes very fast, sometimes very slowly. She was wringing incredible sensations from me with that carefully-regulated infernal back and forth movement.

I cried out stridently every time that mouth swallowed my glans. I pulled her tits out of the brassiere. She moved convulsively and worked my sex around in her wet mouth.

My cock became even stiffer and she realised I was about to come. Kei Ko withdrew her mouth and asked me to lie down on the floor.

I lay on my back, spreading my legs, as requested. A mischievous expression came to her face. She knelt, thighs spread well apart, above my stalk, supporting herself with her hands. She took hold of my tool and used it to separate her lips. Then the lascivious woman moved in such a way that penetration was effected and she remained in that position, crouching over me without touching the rest of my body. Only our sexual organs were in contact and she moved up and down on my stiff sex. The air which her movements created gave me another pleasurable sensation. The alternation of heat and coldness made me even stiffer. She performed that trick-riding stunt like a great sportswoman.

I was at the peak of my pleasure. She accelerated the movements of her vagina which was now very wet indeed. She gave gasping cries as her orgasm approached. I couldn't hold on much longer. The lady asked how things were with me. I retorted that her movements were killing me. She increased her speed again and I could feel myself bumping against the cervix. Then my sex positively exploded, vigorously spraying my come inside her while she sat right down on me, quaking all over. Her hot pussy pumped the last drop of juice out of me. I was exultant.

When Kei Ko got up, my sex was still erect and I wanted to put it in her once more. I got up as well and she said, 'Did you like it in that position? It's very enjoyable for you, but just as much for me too. We call that "The Fluttering Moths", in our books of love.'

'It's an electrifying exercise for the moth and the light which attracts it!'

'Hasn't Migumi shown you all the different positions?'

'She's shown me some of them, but can one say that this oriental classicism is shared by everyone? Anyway, I'm very keen to learn all about them and experience them.'

'You will, soon!'

The more she spoke to me, the more she rekindled my desire. She went into the bathroom and returned carrying a toilet-bag. She placed it on the bedside table and invited me to join her. That's all I was waiting for. Kei Ko asked me to undress her completely, which I did, at the same time massaging her buttocks and hips and sucking her breasts. She felt me to see whether I was stiff enough for her liking, then squeezed my balls and fingered me between the buttocks.

She took a pot of cream from the toilet-bag, opened it, and dipped her fingers into it.

'This cream has a double effect. It lubricates and also amplifies sensations. I'm going to put some on you, then you must put some between my buttocks and in my little entrance.'

The gel which she spread on me took effect quite rapidly. She put plenty on and I began to grow between her agile fingers. She turned over on to her stomach and I insinuated a finger between those shapely buttocks and into the interior, which gave way to my pressure.

After that massage, she got up and moved away from the bed, taking me with her.

I noticed how precisely Kei Ko moved, hips swaying lasciviously, taking long strides, some-times placing her hands on her hips, sometimes behind her head or bringing them down to rest on the two ripe and juicy plums that were her breasts.

She embraced me from the front, then from behind. I followed her movements, the figures of the mannered and sensual dance we were executing. I fingered her vulva, and put my hand in the cleft between her buttocks. She leaned one shoulder against the wall and trapped one of my thighs between hers. She rubbed herself against it, sliding her pubis up and down, sometimes jerking violently.

Her body vibrated against mine as we stood there. I felt her stomach convulsing.

Then she turned away from me, face to the wall, hands resting against it, legs spread. Her body was bending slightly forwards.

'Take me from behind, now! I want to feel your stalk right in me.'

'I'll do my best, Kei Ko. Stick your ass well out.'

She offered her lovely womanly buttocks to me and I guided my cock between them and into the narrow entrance of her pussy. It was slow work, for she was tight. She wasn't relaxed enough yet. I gave another push, then I was inside her velvet sheath. She moaned in pleasure. I fingered her nipples and she began to move her warm little hillocks. As I began to move back and forth, I could feel her buttocks quivering against me. It was nice to watch my organ ramming vigorously in and out and to feel myself gripped so wetly.

She was crying out more and more. She ordered me to go faster. She was driving me crazy. Her convulsions intensified and I was panting all the time now, gripping her tighter and tighter.

'Ah! Ah! Ah! Go on, harder . . . Get the toilet-bag, quickly!'

I turned round and picked it up from the bedside table. I put my hand in and drew forth a steel vibrator which was cold to the touch.

'Have you got it? Quick!'

I played the tip of the enormous object around the opening of her pussy, titillating her clitoris. And I set it going while continuing to thrust my organ in deeply. I was bent right over her. I gave a few more vigorous thrusts between her buttocks. She wanted me to ejaculate. My sperm spurted out and inundated her. She continued to moan and jerk. I went on working her with the vibrator, as she asked me to do.

She surprised me very much, for she came several times over.

'Go on! Put it all the way in and fuck me as hard as you can!'

I withdrew from her wet cunt and gradually inserted the machine. I pushed two fingers into her anus and moved them around in her while the vibrator continued its work in front. After a few minutes like that, she came violently, gasping breathlessly. The lovely woman's whole body was trembling. I turned her round roughly so that she was facing me and pulled her against my sex, which was erect again. Tears of pleasure were coursing down her cheeks.

'Take me standing here against the wall!'

So I did as she desired, pulled her legs up round my hips and slipped into her.

She was suspended from me, my stalk buried up to the hilt inside that juicy pussy. I sprayed her again. Her juices were running down my stomach and my legs. She gave a slight thrust of the buttocks and I took the hint and quickly withdrew!

I released her and lay down on the floor. She joined me there.

'I love to go to the limit of my endurance. It's only then that I really come completely. My muscles contract and I go mad. In a way, it's torture because I get hotter and hotter and it's absolutely necessary for me to be filled back and front.'

My companion went on speaking in the same tone for several minutes, just long enough to enable us to get our breath back. She asked me whether I would like another short encounter.

I said that I would, and she dragged me off to the bathroom.

She got into the bath, drawing me in too by my stalk which, obviously, was erect again. She lightly kissed my member, then told me to be patient for a few seconds. She ran some water. I moved so that it could run on to my prick, which became rather less stiff. She wanted that to happen so that I would be able to piss. When I was ready, she guided my member to her stomach and her pussy, and delighted in it. Afterwards, she turned on both taps and filled the bath. When it was full, she lay down in it, entwining her legs in mine and our sexual organs came closer until they were touching each other. She turned over on her side at a slight angle and took hold of my cock which stiffened rapidly at the touch of those warm fingers.

It seemed a risky position to me.

'It is difficult this way but you get lovely sensations.'

'You're going to hurt my cock like that!'

'Not at all! As soon as it's in, it will follow the shape of my vagina until penetration is complete. Besides, it won't be so hard, but it will rub better and longer.'

'Is this part of the Japanese art of love?'

'It's one of the lighter-hearted variations of the principal figures of the "Unchanging

Attachment" and the "Fishes' Gills Uncovered!" that's not taking cosmic orientation into account, of course!'

'I think it would be better for the moment if we tried to find our sub-aquatic orientation!'

She laughed good-naturedly and so did I, while we were entwining ourselves in an ever-closer embrace.

My stalk penetrated her. We were like two crossed forks. She tightened her grip with her legs and indicated that I should do the same, and we both started to move with an extremely slow and precise back and forth motion. The sensations were all the more pleasing because the bath-water which was moving between us increased the pleasure. She moved, and my cock rubbed against the walls of her vagina. We went on like that for a good half hour before we came superbly, splashing water all over the floor.

The pleasure had been intense and Kei Ko thanked me for my willingness to participate in such a complicated figure. She dried me with a big towel and asked me to get dressed.

When she too had dressed, she offered me a glass of sake. After having drunk it, it was time to leave. She asked me to leave first.

'I have enjoyed our time together very much. I don't think we shall meet again. That's the way things are. Go back to Migumi, the party isn't over yet. She must be thinking that I'm monopolising you.'

I left her and went back down to the great hall. On the first floor, the women were still there standing in front of the doors with their catalogues, then I saw a man emerge looking very pleased with himself and thanking them with Nipponese courtesy.

The party was really gathering momentum. I felt hungry and went over to the buffet. I ate a few canapes and some shrimp fritters and washed them down with a little champagne.

I looked for Migumi and Misako, but couldn't spot them right away. I saw Kei Ko descending the stairs, but she couldn't see me with all these people.

A few moments later, while I was quenching my thirst at the buffet, someone put a hand on my shoulder. I turned round, it was Migumi.

'You were away a long time. Did Kei Ko take you through everything?'

'Just a selection. She revealed a facet of your Japanese erotic art to me.'

'She knows the tradition. Anyway, I'll teach you the rest. I'm going to do you a favour as I can't stay with you.'

'Are you going to allow me to play with Misako?'

'No, not for the moment. She's busy.'

'Then what is it?'

'I'd like you to go up to the first floor. Speak to one of the women there.'

'What do I have to do?'

'Nothing very difficult. The woman wearing a yellow dress is expecting you. She'll show you where to go.'

'I've got to follow the trail?'

'Yes. Nothing simpler. Now I've got to leave you, someone's waiting for me.'

Chapter
6

Migumi disappeared and I went up to the first floor of that manor where I was experiencing the most intense euphoria. My senses revived quickly at the prospect of another erotic encounter. When I reached the corridor which led to the three doors in question, I went up to the woman who was wearing a yellow dress.

I didn't know whether to speak in French or English. When she saw me coming, she greeted me in French. I immediately felt at ease. The Japanese girl offered me a catalogue.

'You will be able to relax now,' she said. 'Here you are, make your choice, please.'

I thanked her and opened the catalogue.

Inside, I discovered the mannequins who had presented the collections at the beginning of the evening. They were all completely naked and had been photographed in very suggestive poses. So I looked through the catalogue, endeavouring to make a choice.

135

I finally picked one who appeared to me to be the youngest. Her name was inscribed at the bottom of the photo: she was called Natsuko.

I showed the picture to the receptionist and waited in the corridor while she disappeared behind a door. She returned a few minutes later and invited me to enter.

When I opened the door, I found myself in a luxurious marble bathroom. To my surprise, a jacuzzi stood in the middle of the room, completely full, with a jet of water continuously playing in its centre. It seemed to be supplied in the same way as the pools in spa towns.

Natsuko appeared, emerging from behind a curtain. She greeted me with a big smile and requested me in English to lie down on a table that was on one side of the room and which I had not at first noticed because of my interest in the superb jacuzzi.

Natsuko undressed me. She was wearing a kimono which revealed a small but firm bosom. When I was lying there completely naked on the massage-table, she began to rub some perfumed oil on her hands. She turned me over on to my stomach and began to massage me.

Her hands relaxed my tense muscles. She continued to speak to me while she was working, asking me if I was feeling less tense and all the time massaging with a precise dexterity which gave me a hard-on.

She lightly slapped my buttocks, massaged them, then turned me on to my back.

I surrendered myself to her totally. She took her kimono off and began to massage my torso. Her breasts brushed against me and the tips hardened.

My stalk was really standing up then. She put some more of the oil on her hands, rubbed them down my thighs and up again to my sex. She took it between her thumb and index-finger and rubbed it. She held my balls in the palm of her other hand, pushed my thighs apart, then ran a warm and agile tongue up my entire length.

That tongue applied light pressures as it moved along, like fingers running over a piano's keyboard.

I was totally relaxed now.

Natsuko requested me to refrain from touching her for a little longer. When the super-subtle, super-sensual massaging was finished, she pulled me into the jacuzzi, where the jet of water continued to dance.

We were in the water together, then she plunged her head under the surface and took my organ into her mouth. The water was very warm, and that increased my excitement. She sucked me like a madwoman while I tried to finger the tips of her breasts. She emerged after two minutes in order to breathe. I couldn't believe my eyes. Then she pulled me close and began to suck me greedily again. The movements of that mouth were giving me exquisite sensations.

I took the young woman by the hips and she came and sat astride me. My stalk penetrated to the very depths of her tight vagina. She twisted against me two or three times, then raised herself. I pulled her close again. Her little games were making me more and more excited. She asked me not to be in too much of a hurry because she wanted to come at the same time as me.

I drew my pretty companion to me and caressed her vulva, then introduced my fingers into her. I kept playing with her clitoris until she began to groan. She put one of her breasts in my mouth and I sucked it for a while, then turned my attention to the other one, sucking each of the sweet little nipples in turn. She nibbled and tongued my ear.

Natsuko indicated to me that she was about to come. So I made her raise her buttocks a bit. I stuck a finger in her ass and worked her back and front.

She wanted to get up and offer me that lovely ass. She supported herself with both hands on the side of the jacuzzi and proferred it magnificently. I took her from behind. My stalk penetrated her tight wet pussy, which gradually opened in response to my vigorous thrusts and her co-operative movements. She swayed and wriggled her hips, moving from one foot to the other in a most exciting way. Then, telling me to hold on tightly, she raised each leg in turn. Thus I achieved deeper and deeper penetration and moved back and forth more easily. My organ seemed to be swelling up strongly inside her.

She began to moan softly, complimenting me on my size. The result was that we both came together, then slipped down into the water.

But my sex remained as stiff as ever. That girl had brought me to a most painful state. I still had a hard-on, and when her hand brushed against my sex, she asked me if I wanted some more. I replied that she ought to suck me to relax me again, as that would soothe my hard-on.

She took me into her mouth and played with my balls. She applied a thumb and index-finger to the base of my stalk and ran them up to the glans which she was sucking energetically.

It was marvellous and I came to my heart's content. She was delighted to have pleased me twice.

I rested in the water for a few minutes. Then I got up and went to get dressed but Natsuko offered to give me one last massage on the table to relax me again. I was delighted.

She massaged me, without oil this time, and my body relaxed. I felt in great shape.

I thanked her. She bowed in the traditional fashion. And I left without asking anything more of her.

When I came out, the lady with the catalogue asked me if everything had been satisfactory. 'More than satisfactory!' I replied. She gratified me with another smile.

When I arrived downstairs, I saw Misako sitting by herself in an armchair. Migumi didn't seem to be around.

In the great hall, there were not so many couples to be seen. I noticed a few men who were being vigorously sucked off in various corners of the room.

I joined Misako. 'I was looking for you a little while ago but Migumi said you were busy,' I said.

'She wanted me to settle a slight problem. It didn't take long. But you disappeared too!'

'I was in the big pool upstairs. Migumi suggested it, but I'd sooner have been with you, Misako.'

'Do you still feel fit after all that?'

'More than that, I feel as if my strength has been doubled!'

'I believe you. Would you like something to drink?'

'Yes please. After all that emotion I'd like a glass of sake.'

She went and fetched me one and offered me a cigarette.

I felt as if I were floating on a cloud, in a dream which seemed to repeat itself indefinitely. Again I saw myself with two new Japanese women who drew me close, offered me their little pussies, who sucked me off, who fluttered around me with a thousand caresses. They were in charge of the programme for the evening and I was in their hands like a prisoner in an undreamed-of paradise.

All these thoughts flitted through my head in a few seconds. I was finishing my sake when a woman motioned to Misako with her hand to go over to her.

She got up, asked me to excuse her, and went over to the woman. When she returned, she proposed that we should have one last drink before leaving.

'Aren't we going to wait for Migumi?' I said.

'No, Migumi will have to stay here until all the guests have gone. She asked me to keep you company.'

'Well, I accept your company with the greatest pleasure. We'll be alone at last, Misako.'

'I'm ready to leave when you are!'

I stood up and we made our way through the dancing couples to the door which led to the entrance-hall. We were given our coats and we left the magnificent building.

As we walked to the car, Misako remained silent. As for me, I was beginning to feel a bit the worse for the mixture of sake and champagne I had drunk. Misako was walking in front of me and I felt like getting a handful of those buttocks which were swaying so temptingly. I restrained myself, however, for some couples were walking towards us. Misako greeted them. They were some of the guests.

Misako opened the door of the Austin and I fell exhaustedly on to the seat.

She drove off rapidly and enquired if all was well with me.

I reassured her. 'It was the coldness when we came out which took me by surprise, that's all. Did you know I've had two baths tonight?'

'I'm not surprised. Did you like Kei Ko? She's a beautiful woman!'

'Very beautiful and very delicate.'

'Would you like to come home with me, Pat?'

'With pleasure. But don't expect much.'

'Don't worry. I'll be as modest as a nun. I just want someone to keep me warm. Tomorrow's a nice easy day. It's Saturday.'

'Already!' I exclaimed. 'I haven't noticed the time passing with you two.'

'You're far too restrictive! You don't know how to count any more, my friend.'

I replied with a smile and a laugh.

We drove along the quays on the banks of the Marne, then we were on the autoroute on our way to Paris.

I began to feel decidedly off colour in the car. Misako was aware that something was wrong.

'What's the matter?'

'I've had too much sake. Would you mind taking me to my place? I need to take something if I'm going to avoid a bad night and a worse day.'

'It's already five in the morning.'

I no longer had any notion of time. Misako promised to look after me when we arrived. I thanked her but didn't want to trouble her. She insisted. That made me feel a bit better.

We arrived in the Rue Tiquetonne, the car stopped in front of the building where I lived. I got out of the Austin quickly, anxious to breathe some fresh air and to walk a bit. I nearly fell, but Misako caught my arm. We went up to the apartment.

She installed me on the bed and brought me the pills I had asked for. She undressed me. I let her do it. That quite excited me, but I couldn't manage to get a hard-on. Everything was out of focus!

'Forgive me, Misako, but I'm in a bad way. We'd better wait till tomorrow.'

'Don't worry, I'm tired out myself. But I'll stay with you until you go to sleep.'

I began to doze off.

Once again I had the same dream in which I saw myself surrounded by a retinue of Japanese ladies all devoted to me. I reached out to touch the superb young women who were doing everything in their power to release me. Then I bumped against Misako, which made me open my eyes to her charming smile. She passed her hand over my forehead, which must have been burning hot. And it was in a burning hot dream that I fell asleep. The Japanese ladies were dancing around me, then I wanted to join in. They excited me and tried to make me get out of bed. The more I tried to approach them, the further away they moved until they disappeared. I made a last desperate effort to hold on to one of them whom I could still see.

The image went hazy. I could no longer see the Japanese ladies and I cried out in despair when the realisation dawned that they had abandoned me.

Chapter
7

I fell out of bed and woke up.

I'd been having a nightmare. I glanced at my watch: it was nine o'clock in the morning. I drank a little of the water which remained in the glass on the bedside table, then fell back into bed, exhausted. I drifted off into a deep sleep.

Consciousness returned to me at about two in the afternoon. A thin ray of sunlight was coming from the sitting room. As I set about preparing some coffee, I found a note from Misako on the kitchen table. She asked me to ring her when I felt better. She'd written down her telephone number.

I drank a few leisurely cups of coffee, then took a shower. Afterwards, I listened to see if my answering-machine had recorded any messages while I had been sleeping. There was nothing. That surprised me. For, since the beginning of my association with Migumi, my main raison d'être had been to hear from her and note her instructions about what was to happen in the evening.

When I was ready, I called Misako. But before doing so, I recalled that Migumi had forbidden me to get in touch with her. I was supposed to wait until one of them established contact. Had Misako been the first one to infringe the rule?

On the phone, I tried to sound light-hearted.

'Are you feeling better now?' she enquired.

'I slept like a log. I had a terrible nightmare, too! I thought you and Migumi had abandoned me. It was too unpleasant for words, and it woke me up. I think I was running a temperature! It was all the emotion last night, at the manor.'

'You must learn how to conserve your strength. It's an art! I'm glad you're better because you've been invited to tea at Migumi's, at five o'clock. I hope you haven't forgotten that Migumi will expect you to give a detailed account of your evening!'

'I won't let her down. Will you be there?'

'Of course. The tea-ceremony will help you.'

She hung up. She seemed very excited, and her voice lingered languorously over the last few words. That revived me.

Before it was time for tea, I strolled around my neighbourhood. I went up the Rue Montorgueil, which was still quiet. I bought some flowers for Migumi and Misako and went back to my place before joining them.

An invitation-card was in my letter-box. I couldn't be bothered to look at the sender's name and put it on my desk among some other papers.

At five o'clock I rang Migumi's doorbell. Misako spoke to me on the intercom and I went up.

She opened the door wearing a lovely open-work dress, which only reached to the middle of her thighs. She closed the door and led the way: her back was bare, apart from two crossed shoulder-straps, and on one side of the dress, below the hips, the fabric, pierced by little round holes, was gathered into flounces. I offered her the flowers. She thanked me.

'Migumi's getting ready,' she said.

'That's a beautiful dress.'

'I've only just bought it. It's quite original, isn't it?'

'It's superb and it fits you perfectly.'

Her lips curved in a smile. She invited me to be seated and then she put some soft music on. I saw that the little tape-recorder was on the table.

Migumi joined us a few seconds later, wearing a black kimono. Her eyes were glittering. Again I found the way she did her hair and make-up disturbing. Her resemblance to Louise Brooks accentuated her doll-like charm.

'I believe you had an enjoyable evening, according to what Misako has told me?'

'Excellent! I didn't feel too good when I got home, but I'd had too much to drink.'

'And was it only drink you'd had too much of?'

'Well, there were some other things too!'

She brought some tea in. She apologised for having neglected me the past few evenings. I replied that the favours she had done me had been a sort of extension of our contract. I was very conscious of that.

Then she asked me to serve the tea.

'While you're serving us, I'd like you to start telling us what happened last night so that we can record it.'

'That will be my pleasure!'

So I served my two Japanese ladies with their tea and began my tale. I told them about the episode with Madame Kei Ko, then about the adventure in the jacuzzi with the mannequin.

While I was relating all that in detail, I was aware of the pleasure that Migumi and Misako took in listening to me. I became very excited myself when I evoked the business about the massage and the cassette with Kathleen. At that point, Migumi interrupted me. 'Did you like the cassette?'

'It was unusual and quite amusing. Kathleen told me that you've got a whole collection of them.'

'That's right. But I would rather teach you something else.'

'For example?'

'Well, the art of preparing oneself for a long night with several women, physical methods of conserving one's sexual fitness, nourishing one's power. . . .'

'And is it applicable to women too?'

'To a certain extent. The woman is the *yin*, the element which extinguishes fire; it is the *yang*, which lights it again, as is shown in *The Book of Changes*. Both of these elements must be present in sexual relations. Those who know the art of *yin* and *yang* can increase their pleasure.'

'I only know an abridged version of it. You're making my mouth water!'

'You must also know how to recognise a woman who is disposed to make love. Without that no communication can be established.'

Migumi was stirring my senses. She was making me quiver with anticipation. I drank some tea to calm myself.

She said, 'Do you feel excited at the moment?'

'Do I look as if I'm indifferent to your teaching?'

'I don't think so. Would you like to quench your thirst by sucking my breasts?' she said suddenly.

I cast a glance at Misako, who turned the music up.

Migumi opened her kimono and picked up a cigarette. I went over to her and started to suck her tits. She only desired my mouth for the moment. I nibbled each of her breasts in turn. My prick woke up and became stiff, straining against my trousers. Migumi threw her head back on the divan and breathed deeply, as if to relax herself. She began to wriggle about as I went on sucking. Her nipples grew stiff and she moaned contentedly. Suddenly she asked me to stop. I obeyed at once.

Then she spoke to Misako: 'It's your turn now, if you like.'

Misako came and sat by me and I held her breasts. She was hot. I sucked them avidly and she reached her peak of pleasure very quickly and began to caress my sex. I felt like taking her clothes off and making love to her. I went to caress her thighs when Migumi intervened.

'Don't be in such a hurry. I'm the one who decides the sequence of our pleasures.'

I listened to her without taking offence. She

was the mistress of the game, I accepted the rules.

Misako got up and changed the music. She put on some of the videos of Prince which she liked so much. She started to dance as the first notes were being played. Migumi seemed excited and sent me into the bedroom to change, where I found a kimono.

When I returned to the sitting room, I found them both dancing sensually, twisting themselves about frantically. Misako moved around her friend, caressing her from time to time, and Migumi was trying to avoid her as in a game. Gradually the ballet began to move in another direction. Migumi began to undress Misako while I watched them, comfortably installed in an armchair. They were making me feel more and more excited.

Misako was now almost naked. She retained her stockings and high-heeled shoes. Migumi danced with her, ass pressed to ass in time with the music. Then she passed a leg between Misako's and moved back and forth against the other girl's well-shaped, active buttocks. Suddenly she turned round to face Misako. They moved close to each other and rubbed their breasts together. Their movements reminded me of certain African dances. I was extremely excited. My prick stood up. I waited for Migumi to invite me to take part in the dance.

Then she looked at me and said, 'I wanted to warm you up a bit. Have you got a good hard-on?'

She came over to me and took off my kimono and revealed how stiff my prick was. She put her arm round me and drew me to the middle of the room. They sandwiched me between them, rubbing themselves against me and bumping their bottoms against me in time with the music.

Misako did a few pirouettes around me. She descended in a movement which evoked the twist of the sixties and briefly licked my stalk. That surprised me and made me laugh and from time to time I licked her breasts as well as Migumi's. Eventually, all that dancing exhausted us.

Migumi told me that these preliminaries were supposed to prepare me for what was to follow. It was essential to conserve my substance for the final figures which she was reserving for Misako and myself.

When we had put our clothes back on, we drank some more tea. Migumi and Misako joked with each other for a few moments in Japanese. Then they burst into joyful laughter and turned their attention to me.

'Do you prefer "The Well-Tied Cicada"?' Migumi demanded.

'Or perhaps "The Rabbit Sucking its Fur"?' Misako continued.

I was astonished by these propositions which conveyed nothing to me.

'All that's Chinese to me. Are they the famous positions I've been hearing about?' I said, laughing.

'Yes. But there are many more, all just as evocative!' Migumi added.

'Am I going to learn them all straight away?'

'No. It will take several evenings, especially as there are two of us to introduce you to them. It will be even more exciting!'

'What instructresses you are! You remind me of the dictum: "A man and woman are like a pair of scissors. One blade is useless without the other."'

Migumi and Misako went to the kitchen to prepare dinner. They left me to my meditations. I was overwhelmed by a delicious feeling of sensual intoxication. I tried to imagine the new positions they had promised to teach me. But undoubtedly their imagination and erotic knowledge far surpassed my own.

We were all wearing kimonos when we sat down at the table. Migumi brought in various dishes of vegetables, rice and raw fish covered with a highly-seasoned sauce. She distributed chopsticks and poured warm sake into our glasses. The alcohol filled me with new life straight away. The food which Migumi and

Misako served me with was light and excellent. I complimented them upon it.

Then we had coffee. Misako put a musical film on and went off to the bathroom. Migumi got up to clear the table and asked me to be patient for a few moments.

She offered me her famous Japanese aphrodisiac cocktail. I drank it with great pleasure. It began to take effect within a few minutes. Migumi went off to join Misako and I heard her arranging her big mirror-screens in the bedroom.

She called me. I entered the room which was bathed in a gentle red and blue light. Misako emerged from the bathroom which adjoined the bedroom. Bandages were wrapped round the tops of her thighs as far as the buttocks. That threw the entry to her sex into relief as well as the opening between the round cheeks of her bottom.

Migumi ordered me to get undressed. She was soon naked herself and came over to feel my rigidity. She and Misako stood on either side of me and spread some of their almond cream on my member.

Misako got into position, hands resting on the bed, buttocks offered. Migumi lay on her back beside Misako, legs pulled well back, offering me her dear little pussy.

'Come and take me, but follow my instructions. Give me six deep, very slow thrusts, then a series of three light thrusts. After that you must take Misako, giving her nine brief thrusts then six deep thrusts. That will increase your pleasure. You must wait until we're wet and make sure your stalk remains nice and stiff. To make your task easier, breathe deeply and have a rest now and again. Your capability will be doubled and your seed will only rise gradually.'

Those instructions were exciting. They were designed to increase the likelihood of the woman having an orgasm and to allow the man to conserve his substance and restrain his orgasm, which could, however, be repeated, as Migumi had indicated.

My task was simple: I had to make them come while refraining from ejaculating during the course of that ceremony in which the thrusts were sometimes even, sometimes uneven. Misako's position gave me sensations which were difficult to control. The sweet little pussy contracted at each penetration. She moved very little during the series of thrusts I gave her. Migumi maintained the position with her legs pulled right back in order to allow me to move about freely inside her. I could feel how wet she was; she wasn't moving much either. My comings and goings between Migumi and Misako achieved epic proportions! It was Migumi who exploded first. She asked me to give short thrusts to prolong her orgasm. Her silken pussy suddenly relaxed its grip.

She guided me with her instructions while I was approaching a paroxysm between Misako's buttocks. I gave a few short thrusts, then some long thrusts. These movements had an immediate effect upon Misako, who squirmed with pleasure and gave a long wailing cry. Migumi made me lie on the bed and installed Misako on top of me, with her back turned towards my face. She sat on my stalk and swallowed it up deep inside her. Migumi supported the young woman's legs and Misako pushed with her hands in order to rise and fall in a series of slow and prolonged movements as Migumi had indicated.

My stalk rubbed against the walls of her vagina and titillated her clitoris. Misako groaned continuously as her buttocks went up and down.

I too started to groan. Migumi asked me if I was about to come. I made it clear to her that Misako's next rapid stroke would make my prick spurt. As the sperm was about to gush forth, Misako got off me and quickly took my stalk into her mouth. The lack of air that I could feel in that mouth, where she held me firmly, increased the intensity of my pleasure. I felt a great sense of relaxation. My muscles slackened and Migumi lifted up my legs while Misako sucked me to the last drop!

I stiffened all over in one last spasm as Misako withdrew. She completed the exercise by rubbing my prick.

Afterwards, Migumi suggested that I should take a bath to relax me. She ran the water and invited me to get in by myself. It did me a power of good.

When I returned to the bedroom, I found that Migumi had set up a big screen there. She told me that she had a series of slides which she would like to show me. I must wait for a while. My gracious hostess brought some drinks into the bedroom and questioned me about the way I had just made love under her guidance. I confirmed that doing it that way made love-making much more exciting.

'One can read about these matters in the best Chinese and Japanese books. The characters of various partners are also described, their physical and moral dispositions as well as what they are seeking in the sovereignty of the sexual act. If the nine spirits of the woman are awake, the man may approach her. It's what you did to us.'

'And how do you know when I'm ready for love?'

'By the way your face muscles relax. Your smile, the disposition of your member, the vibrations of your skin are all so many indications,' Migumi replied.

'And can all this help men with some of their difficulties? I suppose there must be times when a woman isn't up to dealing with a man's excitement, and vice versa.'

'You're right! And that's why I have instituted this ceremony between us. You're aware that I often have to do certain things connected with my work . . . services to render, as Misako has told you. Just lately, pleasure has not been easy to find. Businessmen haven't got a lot of time to spare and they seek strange satisfactions. They demand more than they give. And their practices are in no way original. They leave their signature as on a cheque!'

Migumi went on with her story and recalled our accidental meeting. 'My meeting you was a chance for me to recover my well-being. There was a fifty-fifty chance of that being possible. I could see in your eyes that you seemed disposed to enter into a relationship. Your whole body, your way of moving gave an impression of serenity. Your voice confirmed that first impression. I made up my mind very quickly to keep you with me. The next day, the idea of the contract came to me. I took Misako

160

into my confidence. It was the most certain way of exciting your curiosity!'

She smiled faintly at Misako, who nodded in agreement. My senses stirred again when I looked at that lovely young woman.

It was Misako who continued. 'You know, Migumi is like a sister to me. I've been everywhere with her and our work forms a strong tie between us. These past few years, we've contented ourselves with a few casual affairs, but we've never really had regular boyfriends. Our work just doesn't permit it. When she told me about her evening with you, it aroused my interest and I wanted to meet you. Subsequent events have shown how well we hit it off together. It's made me very happy! What about you?'

'Very happy . . . doubly so?' I replied.

Suddenly, there was a ring at the doorbell. Migumi got up to answer it. Misako confided to me that it was undoubtedly Akiko, the little cousin, who was to join us.

Akiko came into the bedroom where we were waiting for her. She greeted me and glanced at the installation which Migumi had prepared for the slides.

'Sweetheart, Akiko will serve as a model of what you're going to see and reproduce for us. Misako and I will intervene in certain figures.'

'Do I have to prepare myself in any special way?'

'I'll tell you what to do. Just listen to what I have to say after each projection,' she said.

Akiko undressed and slipped into a kimono. Migumi installed the projector to the accompaniment of Misako's and Akiko's laughter. I got on to the bed where Akiko soon joined me. She passed a hand under my kimono and weighed my balls. I caressed her buttocks, which were very firm, and ran my finger round her pussy. Akiko may only have been around seventeen, but the way she behaved indicated quite a lot of experience in sexual matters.

The projector was turned on. The first picture to appear showed one of the most acrobatic positions possible!

Then Migumi asked me to assume a sitting position.

'Akiko, get behind him, and wrap your legs around him. Don't move yet,' she said, addressing herself to me.

Akiko embraced me, then swung forward right over the top of my head. I raised myself up little by little; she was quite light. Then she placed her hands on my thighs to support herself and I held on to her waist.

'Right, now suck each other!'

Akiko took my stalk into her mouth as far as

162

she could get it. She used both hands to help her to rise and fall upon my stiff prick. I thrust my tongue into her little pussy and rubbed her clitoris with my nose. This position had the advantage of offering the body absolutely and enabling each of the partners to concentrate on helping the other to reach the peak of excitement. Akiko was moving my penis around in her mouth and I was thrusting my tongue into her ever more vigorously. Migumi and Misako thought we were doing quite well.

'Are you both thoroughly aroused?' Migumi demanded.

It was difficult to reply quickly. She came over to us and put an end to our sucking. Akiko stood up and I replied that indeed I was thoroughly aroused. She too caressed me and observed that my stalk was still nice and stiff.

'We'll look at some of the others now. You can stay on the bed if you like,' she said.

Misako came over to join me and massaged me a little on the thighs, in the small of the back and the shoulders to relax the muscles.

Migumi projected the slides, every time telling me the pleasing names of the positions. One was called 'A Couple of Swallows', a classic position in which the woman raises one of her legs to allow deeper penetration; another was called 'The Dance of the Two Female Phoenix.'

'This one's interesting.' Migumi pointed out. 'You can do it. Misako and Akiko will be your two phoenix.'

Misako lay on her back and asked Akiko to lie on top of her. Akiko made Misako spread her legs and arranged herself so that their vulvas were close to each other. Misako's bare pussy was gaping open and Migumi ordered me to place myself opposite those two portals of pleasure.

I turned my attention to Akiko's little pussy first and pushed my cock deeply into her. Then I entered Misako's warm and welcoming cunt. I passed from one to the other but only giving a certain number of thrusts as decreed by Migumi who, at the same time, was caressing my buttocks. Sometimes I would give a series of brief thrusts, sometimes a series of slow ones. Each of my withdrawals, in order to pass from one portal to the other, increased the size of my erection. Sometimes Akiko guided me with her thumb and forefinger.

We had to remain in that position and I had to keep to the series of thrusts which Migumi had imposed on me. My purpose was to try to make the girls come first. It wasn't long before Akiko was wet and gasping. I felt my seed rising and I was breathing heavily. Misako was pressing my cock from below. The pleasure intensified. Misako was as wet as could be now, and my final thrusts wrung desperate groans from her. She squeezed her thighs together and I shot my load into her receptive vagina as if I would never finish. We came together. I flopped down between the two of them. Migumi complimented us and came over to the bed where she gave me her breasts to suck.

I sucked that juicy fruit to quench my thirst while Akiko massaged my buttocks. Misako turned round then and occupied herself by gently stroking my sex. Then I felt two tongues disputing which should have the right to lick my prick. Hot and cold waves ran through my whole body. Those mischievous caresses set me quivering so much that I felt as if my circuits were bursting like bubbles! Three Japanese girls were suspended above me, sucking me greedily! It was out of this world! They tickled me as they sucked my nipples. I roared. They each took turns in licking my balls. I tried to put my fingers in Migumi but she kept out of reach. I reached out for Akiko. She came and gave me her nipples to suck. They were like the points of well-sharpened pencils.

Then Migumi asked me to stand up and finger her as well as Misako. And at the same time I was to take their breasts into my mouth.

She made Akiko come between us, she knelt at my feet and took me in her mouth. The task was not easy. The girls were extremely excited.

Migumi told Akiko to rub herself against my leg so that she could come too.

We all achieved satisfaction quickly. There was still a last drop on the top of my glans but my stalk remained erect because of the sucking it had received! Migumi was delighted for, according to her, I was ready to proceed to the other positions.

Akiko served us some more drinks and brought in some fruit.

After that short interlude, Migumi returned to the projector. Couples reproduced famous Japanese prints and adopted every conceivable position. The pictures succeeded each other in an atmosphere of good humour. The girls kept laughing heartily.

While a pose involving a rather fat woman was on the screen, Migumi informed me that the position was called 'The Phoenix Holding its Chick' in the classical manuals. The expression made me laugh, for the man was of small stature and about to shaft a woman of considerable weight, and he was guiding his member to the portal for fear that it might lose its way!

The scenes became more and more irresistible. Migumi said that it would be best to realise them another time as they required an adequate and precise preparation of body and mind.

The pictures were exciting us. Migumi asked Misako to put her musical videos on and poured me a glass of sake. They drank some too.

Migumi came close to me and said, 'I'm going to pour a little sake on your sex, it will keep you in good shape.'

She took some sake into her mouth and put some on my glans, which she sucked with great delicacy. The effect was electric, I tingled a bit but her mouth soon made that impression disappear. Misako and Akiko did the same, which made me even stiffer. My blood boiled and my temples throbbed.

The three Japanese ladies lay down on the moquette. Migumi asked me to suck all of them.

I started with Misako, who didn't have a fleece and upon whom my tongue slid perfectly. I separated the lips of her vulva and started to lick her clitoris. Then I turned my attention to Migumi, who gripped my head in order to make me lick her more deeply. She was the first one to cry out. Next, it was Akiko's turn. She opened her thighs as widely as possible to make it easier for me to use my tongue, which I did, thrusting it into her with diabolical energy. I lingered over Akiko, for I could feel her quivering all over. Her pussy had fine, resilient lips which retracted at each stroke of my tongue.

Migumi wanted to be bitten, so I nibbled her stiff little bud. I took it between my teeth and made it dance a lascivious funk, like the black dancers we saw on Misako's videos. I followed the rhythm of 'Delirious', coming and going between her loins. She cried, 'Not yet!'

'You've become an expert!' Misako sighed.

'It's your doing! And I like it!' I replied.

I went back to her and made her groan to her last breath. She was soaking wet with pleasure and pulled away from me, twisting and writhing. Akiko was the last, with Migumi, who wailed wildly.

Akiko got up first. She went to get the pot of cream and put some between her legs. She came to me and massaged my prick with creamy fingers. She positioned herself, buttocks pointed towards my stalk. I started to open her little by little. She gave a loud cry. I withdrew and put a bit more cream on her, pushing my finger into the little opening of her pussy in an attempt to enlarge it.

Migumi made the girl put her hands on the wall and open her legs. Misako lightly massaged her breasts. Then I began the task of penetration again, going at it as gently as possible from behind while Migumi and Misako stood on each side of me, stroking my bottom and slipping their fingers between Akiko's buttocks and my stiff tool, which was moving in

168

and out very slowly. Misako caressed my balls. At the same time Migumi was running her tongue along the entire length of my spine. The sensations intensified. The electricity spread to the centre of my skull. It went between my eyes, down my nose, through my stomach to the sex organ itself. I was now giving stronger thrusts into Akiko's tight entrance and she had started to wiggle responsively. In fact, she moved about with such vigour that she ended up by coming, so I accelerated my thrusts in order to give her complete satisfaction.

I still had a good hard-on, and now it was Migumi's turn. I pulled the cheeks of her bottom open with my hands and thrust myself deeply into her cunt from the rear. She told me to give a series of nine slow thrusts, then a series of six faster ones, which I did with indescribable joy. I slid in and out with the greatest ease, and she even danced a few steps. I followed her, trying not to become dislodged. Misako helped us in that frolic. Several times she held my sex, rubbing it between her thumb and forefinger. That little game made my stalk as stiff as possible.

Migumi asked me if I were going to ejaculate in her. I replied that she would have to move about a bit more, and more vigorously. Then she commanded me to give her three rapid thrusts followed by eight long, deep ones. That brought me close to orgasm but I still managed to hold on. I wanted to make her come before I did. The increasing loudness of her moans made me realise that she was on the verge of orgasm. She literally collapsed under my final thrusts. I was soaking wet with her juices. She invited me to possess Misako, if I still felt capable of doing so.

Misako positioned herself. She too was very wet. She applied some more of the cream to both of us. I took her quickly and slid straight in. She opened up like a ripe fruit. We moved together in a sustained and regular rhythm. From time to time she made spasmodic movements with her ass. At that moment, Migumi intervened to insist that Misako should win the competition by making me ejaculate. Misako redoubled her thrusts while I squeezed her breasts and pulled and twisted the nipples. This excited her almost beyond endurance. She gave long moaning cries as I moved her around on my shaft. I made as if to pull it right out, then thrust right back into her, making her come. I couldn't restrain myself any longer. Misako's jerks made the volcano erupt! I twisted about and pulled her up against me. I was panting and gasping furiously. I was absolutely exhausted, drained of all my seed, totally satisfied.

Migumi and Akiko applauded and welcomed us on the bed where they gently massaged us.

It had been a hard-fought game, no doubt about that!

We drank some fruit-juice to quench our thirst. Migumi decided that it was time for the party to end. We got dressed and had one last glass of sake in the lounge.

Misako left first as Migumi had previously decided she would. We said goodbye to each other. Akiko, the young cousin, remained with Migumi. She was extremely docile, and very polite. She thanked me profusely for an enjoyable evening. I expressed my gratitude for the pleasure I had received and which she had given me.

Migumi reminded me of the clauses of the contract before I left. More precisely, she said that I was to wait for a call from her. I thanked the young woman for revealing a new facet of Japanese and Chinese erotic art to me. She congratulated me for having proved myself to be more than equal to the demands of three greedy girls.

I gave her one last smile as I left the apartment. She bowed to me then blew me a kiss. I was very surprised!

Chapter
8

I didn't understand the meaning of her gesture until later. That evening, I thought our fabulous union had made her decide to open even more intimate doors to me. For that I thanked the conjunction of the *yin* and *yang* and the 'Unchanging Attachment' to the principles of Japanese erotic art.

Eros, the master of the frolics of the 'Fluttering Ducks', accompanied me in my sleep and made me relive the stately dance of the honey-lipped daughters of the Rising Sun.

On Sunday, I woke up very late in the afternoon. I drank several cups of coffee and put on a record of Anita O'Day singing 'Trav'lin' Light'. I had the feeling that I was about to start another night of delights. I dressed and went out to get some fresh air.

I installed myself in a café near the Opéra, watched the passers-by and flipped through some magazines. I inspected the other tables:

there weren't many other people there. The sound of voices grew progressively louder as time passed. I had finished the tea which I'd ordered.

I glanced distractedly at the faces of the other customers as I leafed through a magazine. Suddenly two women entered the café. One was Japanese and seemed to me to be Natsuko, who I had met at the manor-house the other night. She was accompanied by a platinum blonde. They looked for a place to sit and found one not far from my table. I fixed my eyes on Natsuko, who recognised me almost immediately. She greeted me enthusiastically and introduced her friend, who was American. I invited them to have a drink. Natsuko thanked me but declined because she had something to discuss with her friend. She promised to join me a bit later.

When she accepted my invitation, I wondered if she was bound to Migumi in secrecy like Misako was. Perhaps they didn't work together? I turned over all the possibilities in my mind, and one in particular: that of spending another evening with her. The memory of her massaging me came into my mind. I quivered. An afternoon of being caressed by those hands . . . but undoubtedly I was letting my imagination run away with me as I leafed through my magazine.

Eventually the American woman left.

Natsuko came and sat at my table. 'I didn't want to involve my friend in our conversation . . . you understand?' she said in English, with her delightful accent.

'Yes, of course. Did it embarrass you to meet me here?'

'Oh no, not at all!' she replied very serenely.

'You know Migumi, of course?'

'Yes. I'm only in Paris for a few days. I'm based in London and Tokyo, of course. Migumi makes all the arrangements for accommodation and receptions when we give fashion-displays. I have quite a lot of freedom of choice, actually. I've only been working for this agency for a few months, but everything's fine so far.'

'Do you often do jobs for it apart from modelling?'

'Sometimes, but I'm free to refuse. The other evening was an exception. I found the idea amusing! And you?'

'I was surprised. Meeting you was very exciting. My body still bears the imprint of your fingers!' I said, laughing.

She laughed too. I sensed that she was as hot as I was. Her shoulders were quivering imperceptibly. The expression in her eyes when she looked at me spoke louder than words.

177

'Would you like to come and have an aperitif at my place? It's only a few steps away.' I said.

She was delighted with the idea.

As we left the café, I had a moment of apprehension, but quickly recovered. After all, perhaps my fears were unjustified. I wondered whether there would be a message from Migumi on my answering-machine. In that case, my evening with Natsuko would be curtailed. And how would Migumi react if she learnt about this second and unexpected encounter with one of her models? Would she have brought her into our splendid contract?

We cut through the Place des Victoires and went along the Rue Étienne-Marcel. We passed Rue Montorgueil and entered the Rue Tiquetonne. Natsuko wasn't familiar with this part of the city. I told her a bit about its history. And then we arrived at my apartment.

'What would you like to drink?'

'Have you got any gin?' she said.

I gave her a glass of gin and had a Martini myself. It was barely six o'clock in the evening. There were no messages on the answering-machine.

I drained my glass and sat down beside Natsuko. I didn't have time to slip my hand under her skirt before she unzipped me and brought out my prick, which was already stirring.

She went no further but asked me what I wanted. That took me somewhat by surprise. I asked her what she wanted. She replied that if I would like her to take charge as she had done the other night, that was no problem; an answer which suited me perfectly.

First of all she undressed me then took off her dress and underclothes. She made me lie down on the sofa and licked my stiff prick a few times. I caressed her breasts while she was positioning herself. I found myself face to face with a beautiful firm, rounded ass. When she started to suck me, I was already exploring her agile pussy with my tongue. I gripped her hips and ran my tongue along that soft flesh. I reached the little bud and took it between my teeth. She was sucking me more and more strongly. My stalk went right into her throat, which seemed to have an infinite capacity. She was taking her time, nibbling me and moving right back up to the glans, then descending as if she was unrolling a velvet carpet. I tried to adjust myself to my partner's rhythm and felt myself to be growing enormously stiff. She withdrew her mouth from my stalk.

Then Natsuko made me spread my legs slightly apart and came on top of me with her back towards me. She quickly introduced my prick into a warm and welcoming vagina. She brought her knees together and, using both hands for support, made the elevator of voluptuousness rise and fall. She went right to the top floor, then descended slowly and deeply. Her juices were beginning to flow, and she was getting warmer and warmer.

'When I come down next time, thrust upwards hard,' she said.

I did straight away, which caused her to gasp and groan more and more. That set me going. I cried out with pleasure as my stalk buried itself deeply within her. She asked me if I were going to come. I replied that the way we were going on it wouldn't be long. Then she started to move faster. I did the same and gave harder thrusts. She bounced up and down on top of me, and we kept going until orgasm overwhelmed us. Natsuko sat right down on my stalk as the hot sperm emptied into her depths! She relaxed and lay down on top of me. I put my arms around the young woman's breasts and wound my legs round hers. We stayed like that for several minutes. Then she took my hand and placed it on her wet, warm, open pussy. She guided my fingers to the vulva and made me rub it lightly but continuously. She began to come endlessly. My prick woke up between her buttocks and she led it to its destination again. She ran the glans back and forth between the vaginal lips, concentrating especially on the little bud. It was a very pleasant exercise. I came once more, all over her stomach. She seized my stalk and rubbed it vigorously. I rubbed her too until she achieved satisfaction.

Natsuko got off me and said some sweet and playful things to me. She was a very affectionate girl. I paid her some compliments. The young woman's smile was an eloquent way of saying thank you.

I offered her another drink, which she accepted. She got dressed and asked what time it was.

It was a quarter past seven by my watch. 'Are you in a hurry?' I said.

'Somewhat. I've been invited out to dinner. It's a pity.'

'It can't be helped. Anyway, I've got to go out myself later tonight,' I replied, to put her at her ease.

She gave me a charming smile. I passed my hand over her buttocks, as a sign of regret. That amused her. She stayed for a few more minutes. When she got up to go, Natsuko told me that we would not be able to meet again as she was leaving Paris, and that it was perhaps for the best.

'It's a pity!' I replied.

Nevertheless, she gave me a big smile when she left. Those Japanese girls really were terribly seductive!

All the time I had spent with Natsuko had left me with a bitter-sweet taste at the back of my throat. I didn't know why that was. My life had taken a strange direction these last few nights. I had been following just one rule: to let myself be carried along by the pleasurable eroticism of my ardent Japanese ladies!

Time passed. I drank Martini after Martini and listened to music. I had a light meal.

At nine-thirty the telephone rang. It was Migumi. 'How are you today?'

'Very well. I've recovered my strength. I come alive as soon as it's night.'

'Would you like to come to a small, informal party?'

'To continue our course of instruction upon "The Unchanging Attachment"?'

'In a way. I'll teach you to pluck my "Chords of the Lute" in the traditional way.'

'As a musician, I am your humble servant!'

We hung up and I went round to her place.

When she let me in I had a surprise. The apartment was more than usually tidy, various things had disappeared from the sitting room, and bouquets of flowers, the sophisticated *ikebana*, decorated the four corners of the room. Migumi was wearing traditional costume.

I noticed that Misako was not there. Had

that been arranged by Migumi so that she could be alone with me? But undoubtedly Misako could appear at any minute, according to a scenario devised by Migumi.

She offered me a cup of coffee and warmed some sake. She lavished attention on me and spoke about the new collections which were keeping her busy at the moment. She seemed to have a number of things on her mind but she didn't say anything about them. After we'd had our coffee, she went and fetched a book for me to look at. It was written in Japanese but there were numerous illustrations. It was a classical erotic manual embellished with ancient prints and woodcuts.

She translated certain passages which were written in a picturesque style whose terms were mannered but very evocative.

Then she wanted to begin the ceremony. She asked me to put on the kimono that she had prepared for me, which I did without delay. Underneath it I was completely naked.

She asked me to sit cross-legged, and made me drink a little warm sake. She sat facing me and drew closer, pressing her knees against mine. My stalk began to wake up under the kimono. She took it in her hand and began to rub it. While it was stiffening, she applied her lips to the glans, then sucked it, running a tongue still burning from the sake around it.

She passed her hands under my buttocks and drew me closer with slow and regular movements. My stalk disappeared into that sucking mouth and my balls began to tingle. The excitement made me withdraw slightly.

Then she left it standing up in the air and said, 'Now that you're ready, we'll try some more positions. We'll start with "The Monkey Embracing a Tree and Groaning".'

That made me laugh heartily!

I remained sitting cross-legged and Migumi came and crouched over my lap. She put one hand under my buttocks and used the other to introduce my stalk into her invitingly open pussy. When she was well and truly impaled, she put her arms around me. I used one hand to support myself and the other to move her rhythmically up and down, while she raised herself by pushing with both feet. We soon found the right rhythm and were completely united. That position gave me immense pleasure. We moved faster. Her breasts bounced and her buttocks danced on me. We came together with great voluptuousness.

My education continued with another position: 'The War-Horse Galloping'. Migumi showed me what to do.

She lay on her back, I drew her head to me with my left arm and made her bring both feet up to her buttocks. Migumi's body now formed a geometrical angle, an absolutely pliable geometrical angle! I lowered myself and aimed my well-greased, quivering stalk between the proffered buttocks. I penetrated her easily, then followed her directions.

I had to bend my partner's body from time to time so that her head and legs were raised alternately. Migumi's lightness was a great help in that position. My prick moved smoothly in and out and Migumi pursued her odyssey of sexual harmony. While she told me about the benefits of these practices, I was thrusting away rhythmically inside her. She thrust back at me responsively. She had a spasm of pleasure after a series of slow strokes. And my stalk seemed to grow and grow. In that delightful position, our pleasure was increasing all the time. She extolled the five senses of the woman who is inclined to make love and the various movements a man could make to satisfy all those senses. The more she revealed of those practices to me, the more excited I became deep inside her. We timed it so that we came together and the orgasm nearly took my breath away. I lay down between her thighs, my head resting on her breasts.

It was an intensely exciting session. Her words and what she described while we were fucking had an electrifying effect on me. I had a vision of a thousand Japanese ladies who were caressing me delightfully and giving themselves to me in a multitude of inviting positions. That only increased my desire.

Migumi was extremely voluptuous that evening. She made me choose some positions too. I opted for 'The Bamboos Near the Altar'.

I wanted to add a bit of spice to the position in question. She was willing. So I took her to her famous exercise-bar and made her stretch both arms out horizontally. We were facing each other and I put my arms round her, then rubbed myself against her vulva while nibbling both nipples, which were becoming stiffer. I made her spread her legs then and asked her to hold on tightly to the bar with both hands. She gripped it and I started to enter her, moving the glans from left to right to separate the vaginal lips, then I slid right inside. At that moment, I lifted her up by her legs while she flexed her hands. She evidently approved of my procedure.

'We could reconsider the whole series of classical positions and modernise them to suit the furniture! Don't you think so?' she said.

Migumi was moving about a lot. My organ rose and fell in her vibrating lute chords.

When we arrived at the point of orgasm, she relaxed and I pulled her to me, liberating her from the bar. She squeezed my stalk in one last contraction of the vaginal muscles. That made me come straight away and she too exploded, her whole body shaking, arms gripping me convulsively.

I gave her everything I'd got and the wetness sent shivers along my spine. We were steaming with voluptuousness and our bodies gave one last violent shudder. I carried her over to the bed and we lay down together.

My evening with Migumi ended after a little more sucking and a bath, which we took together. I left as agreed.

The days which followed were more and more eventful. Migumi invited me over in the afternoon mostly, because she was often not available in the evening. Misako frequently joined us. She assisted Migumi several times in our sensual frolics.

My life took a new direction. I wound up my outstanding business with a record-company. I no longer bothered to read letters which were sent to me by various girlfriends, who couldn't get me on the telephone either. I never replied to their messages. It would have been too complicated for me. I gave myself entirely to Migumi. I couldn't imagine a better way of amusing myself or attaining pleasure. Every time I met a Japanese woman in the street, I got a furious hard-on. Memories flooded my mind and I imagined them waiting for me at Migumi's door.

One evening it was Misako who took charge of the ceremony of pleasures, and we spent the whole night drugged by sake and the most profound sensuality.

Sometimes I arrived late and had to pay various forfeits to satisfy my two ladies.

On such occasions, they would send me to change as soon as I arrived. I would put on the kimono which was reserved for my use. And I served them according to a ritual devised by Migumi. I brought them tea first of all, put the various dishes for our dinner on to a big tray in the kitchen and carried it to the low table in the sitting room. I would put a bit of music on when they asked me to. And they took it in turns to say things to me.

'Do you get a hard-on when you brush against us?' Migumi demanded.

'Would you like to be sucked now?' Misako enquired.

I was never allowed to reply. They confined me to a silence in which only my gestures could express my feelings. Then they would play some games with me: I had to suck their breasts, at the same time keeping a certain distance between us. They took a mischievous pleasure in seeing my sex grow and pop out of the kimono from time to time.

Migumi often used the chopsticks to play with my cock which stood up when I approached her to suck her juicy, swollen nipples!

'Well! Here's a fluttering butterfly which has a very big stalk for its body!' she would say laughingly.

Misako would approach then, and take my stalk between the chopsticks and amuse herself by dexterously manipulating me. It was tremendously exciting. My stalk stood up between those skilfully handled chopsticks. Then they would suddenly stop.

I would be left standing there in a state of unsatisfied desire which they had aroused in me, my stalk sticking up in the air. Then suddenly Migumi would get up and greedily take it into her mouth.

They often played such games with me. Then, if I had served them satisfactorily, they would accord me all kinds of favours.

Every evening, things got a bit spicier. When Misako arrived late, I had to finger her as she stood there, arms folded behind her back, while Migumi made her spread her thighs and held them so that she couldn't move. That wrung torrid spasms from Misako, convulsing her whole stomach. She went rigid and groaned louder and louder as my fingers did

189

their work. Migumi lightly slapped her friend's buttocks to accelerate the orgasm.

When Migumi was in a joyful mood, she would ask us to take her. She would make me sit on a chair, then I would introduce my stalk from behind and finger her energetically in front. Misako caressed her friend's breasts, and bit them when she was asked to do so.

On certain occasions, one or the other would wrap her legs around my hips and I had to do it like that, standing up, walking or dancing according to whatever music Misako played. They wriggled about like babies and I had to keep my balance and move my stalk carefully. Migumi would then suggest a series of extremely rapid thrusts as we were dancing. My organ plunged deeply into her at an infernal speed.

Every time, we separated very late in the night. In the morning, I would wake up feeling stiff in every joint. So I got into the habit of doing some gymnastic exercises. They soon got me into better shape.

In the days which followed, I went to Migumi's apartment less frequently. Misako would phone me and postpone our rendezvous until a later date because of a last-minute business meeting.

During such periods of calm, I would

daydream about 'The Flight of the Seagulls' or the 'Mandarin Ducks'. There was never an afternoon when my penis did not stir and stand up in expectation of a night of sensuality and sake.

Migumi would often defer our meetings and suggest that I should take Misako out to dinner, then she would come and join us towards the end of the meal. After that, we would go back to her place.

I frequently had the pleasure of bathing her and putting cream on her body. She and Misako were making my life more and more exciting. They were attentive to my every wish.

One weekend, Migumi decided to go to Trouville. We set off with Misako. The journey was as exciting as could be. We took to the road on Friday evening.

There was a tape-deck in Migumi's car. She put on a cassette like the one Kathleen, her American friend, had played to me.

Migumi drove. The tape played. And she asked me to follow the cassette's instructions. The game excited her. She desired at all costs to experience the same emotions as Kathleen when she had done it with me on the ring-road.

But this game was harder to play. The roles were reversed. It was up to me to take the initiative and, first of all, to take off the skirt she was wearing as well as her panties.

I fingered her vigorously. Then I removed the skirt, all the time feeling her buttocks. It fell down to her ankles as she was driving. She rid herself of it expertly, pressing alternately on the pedals of the car. Sweat stood out on my forehead. Misako watched what was happening, clutching the seat.

The cassette played on. I found it easier to remove Migumi's blouse and I continued to finger her. When she was completely naked and well warmed-up, she asked me to move over to her seat.

We were on the autoroute, it was about ten o'clock at night.

She moved forward a little, moving one buttock after the other. I had to slide on to the seat by lifting her up a bit in order to get my leg across, then wedge my foot near the pedals, without distracting her attention from the road.

Suddenly, my foot slipped on to the accelerator. Misako and Migumi screamed! I thought that we were going to crash. For, at that moment, I couldn't see what was happening in front of us. I immediately withdrew my foot while Migumi braked a little. The danger was over.

I was right under Migumi, legs apart, trousers down. Fear had cooled our passion. At that moment, how fast we were going was of more interest to me. But I started to caress her again, and the contact with Migumi's bare buttocks soon restored my hard-on. My fingers sought her pussy again, to warm her up once more. Then she wanted to sit on my stalk, which had reassumed its full stature. I lifted her up and, with a well-timed movement, slid deeply into the warm depths. So far, so good, but she wanted more. I had to move rhythmically in and out without making her go too wild. We were moving at at least ninety kilometres per hour. The faster my movements became, the more she tended to accelerate. I held her by the hips and skilfully moved her up and down. Migumi began to feel a storm rising in her vagina. She spoke excitedly in Japanese and Misako laughed loudly. She was groaning more and more, which reassured me, for my orgasm was fast approaching and my limbs were quivering tensely. I had to go carefully, though, so that she wouldn't lose control of the car. Migumi was no longer afraid at all. The only thing that mattered to her now was having a good orgasm. It mattered to me too! I was aware that she was going a bit faster. The car moved along as straight as an arrow.

Migumi's body was quivering all over and I could feel my juice rising. I told her, which had the effect of making her come straight away. Simultaneously, she put her foot down on the accelerator. Then I grabbed the wheel with one hand, for we were going excessively fast. She went completely limp, and nearly lost control of the car as she lifted her foot from the accelerator.

After all that, we drew in to the side of the road and stopped for a while. Migumi was delighted with the experience. She told me it was the first time she had ever done that.

We set off again with Misako driving. When we reached Trouville, we celebrated our joy-ride at a restaurant called *The Steamers near the Harbour*.

Migumi said she was willing to grant me a favour that night. At the hotel, we took a room for three, which somewhat shocked the lady at the reception-desk.

All I demanded of Migumi and Misako that night was a simple massage-session, to help me unwind after so much emotion. They satisfied my desire in accordance with the rules of the art, and with great subtlety.

When I closed my eyes, more images surged into my over-excited brain. My nerves raced wildly in my skull, blotting out the rhythm of my pulse. I drifted off into a series of the strangest dreams. Visions of women in the throes of orgasm alternated with faces seen in night-clubs where I sometimes went on particularly depressing evenings. Then suddenly, a strong light seemed to draw me from my sleep. And, without any logical progression, I was transported to a garden where a thousand fans danced while I lay on a car seat. Hands full of ardent desire ran over my body, which was avid for sensations. And I was experiencing inexpressible delight.

For me, those parties with Migumi and Misako were events the like of which I had never before experienced, truly memorable occasions in my life.

The return journey from Trouville to Paris was less epic, although very delightful. We took it in turns to drive and to sit on the back seat. Migumi had the bright idea of playing the cassettes of the accounts I had given of my special missions! They gave her a very real pleasure and she was all the more demanding with me. As was Misako!

Chapter
9

During the week which followed our trip to Trouville, my experiences of Chinese and Japanese eroticism continued. On several occasions I was 'The Leaping White Tiger' or 'The Monkey in the Third Moon of the Springtime'.

On certain evenings, Akiko, the young cousin, received me and we waited for Migumi, who had been detained by business matters. She dressed me in traditional costume. I put on a *hakama*, which was like a pair of wide-legged trousers, and wore it with a kimono. She served me a drink and prepared the dinner.

When Migumi arrived, she was always radiant and took charge of the proceedings with a perfect receptiveness of mind. She herself organised the ritual of our pleasures. And to show how sorry she was for being late, she would pay me some forfeits. I would remember our first meeting and ask for a double aperitif:

sitting cross-legged, she would suck me when dinner was finished. Sometimes I took her in front of the exercise-bar in her bedroom. She would rest against it like a doll and let me do whatever I liked. I would play with her, moving her around in every direction.

Thus I spent my nights, a prisoner of her desires and her art of living.

For me the days were often long preparations for my nights with Migumi. I awaited her orders and only picked up the telephone in the hope of hearing her voice.

Sometimes our meetings were postponed. We would arrange to meet at one o'clock in the Champs-Élysées to have lunch together. Migumi would be making arrangements for a new presentation of her collections in various foreign salons, which took up an enormous amount of her time as well as Misako's. The lunches were a kind of apology, her way of asking me to be patient.

Then my evenings became monotonous. I did the round of the night-clubs or hung around in certain cafés.

Five days went by without any news from Migumi. On the sixth day, I received a call from Misako. 'We're both terribly sorry about this long silence. Could you come to the café at about four o'clock? Migumi is extremely busy.

200

I'll explain everything to you . . .'

'But what's happening with you two? Is Migumi there?'

'No. Come to the café near the agency, I'll tell you all about it.' That was all Misako would say, then she hung up.

I got ready to go to my rendezvous. When I arrived in the Rue La Boétie, I installed myself at a table in the café with a few minutes in hand.

Half an hour went by and Misako had still not appeared. I had learnt the art of being patient with my two Japanese ladies. Sometimes surprising things ended up happening to me. An hour ticked away. My anxiety grew. I watched the door of the agency, which was opposite the café. Still nothing.

At six o'clock, I'd had two coffees and a Martini and Misako still hadn't turned up. I was somewhat on edge with all that waiting, which seemed to me to bode no good.

I left the café and went over to the entrance of the building. I looked at the plaques and tried to find the name of Migumi's agency. There was nothing there which even remotely resembled a Japanese name. But I noticed that a plaque was missing.

I went in and looked for the caretaker. When I unearthed him, I felt a bit embarrassed about asking him whether there had ever been a Japanese fashion agency in the building. He replied that they had moved three weeks previously. I was completely taken aback, but didn't let him see it. I told him that I must have got the wrong address and left. I went back to the café and looked inside. No sign of Misako. And no agency either, now!

I went straight back to my place as fast as possible.

There were no messages on the answering-machine. Had Misako been prevented from coming at the last moment? Was she waiting for a message from Migumi? Was it a new game which they had decided to play with me? I turned all these questions over in my mind as I paced up and down in my apartment.

At eight o'clock there was still no message. Suddenly, I recalled that Misako had given me a piece of paper with her telephone number written on it. It was the evening she came home with me after that memorable party in the manor house. I remembered that feeling of having been hit on the head with a bamboo pole, the result of mixing sake and champagne.

I looked everywhere in the kitchen, and found nothing. Then I hunted through all the papers and letters which were heaped on my desk in indescribable disorder. I wouldn't go to Migumi's apartment, for I respected her contract. The situation was intolerable to me. My desk was in danger of collapsing as a result of

202

my frenzied search. Then, wedged between two invitation cards, I found Misako's note together with her telephone number which she had left for me.

I dialled the number, all sorts of inconsequential thoughts whirling around in my head. A recorded voice answered, 'The number you are dialling has been disconnected . . .' I slammed down the receiver, then tried again, to make sure there was no mistake about it. The recorded voice repeated its depressing message.

I spent a night without a 'Flight of Seagulls' or any 'Fluttering Moths'. My dreams were haunted by elusive Japanese ladies who promised a paradise of delights always postponed until later.

The next day, I got up very early. Once more I went to the café where Misako was supposed to have met me. I only stayed there for a few moments, then took a walk round that quarter. Nothing to be seen.

I decided to look for the telephone numbers of Japanese fashion agencies in a trade directory, a plan which proved to be unsuccessful.

Then I spent the day walking around all the quarters of Paris. I lingered in the area around the Opéra and returned home at eight o'clock in the evening.

I didn't know whether to arm myself with patience and wait for a sign from my two

Japanese ladies or perhaps to take a chance and go to Migumi's apartment. I decided to wait one more night.

The following day, I walked past the building where Migumi had her apartment and looked at the windows. There was no sign of a living soul. I didn't dare ring her door bell, so I went on my way. When night came, I began to pace up and down my sitting room, waiting for the telephone to ring. The hours seemed interminable.

At eleven o'clock, I couldn't bear it any longer. I had to find out what was going on. I left my apartment and went round to Migumi's place.

I rang her bell. A few moments later, a voice answered in Japanese. It was neither Migumi's nor Misako's. Nervous tension made it difficult for me to speak at first, then I asked, in English, if Migumi were there. The unknown woman didn't reply but opened the door. I took the lift, and a few seconds later found myself on the floor where Migumi's apartment was situated.

A Japanese lady who I had never seen before appeared. She was wearing a kimono and must have been between thirty-five and forty. Her extremely made-up face broke into a smile. She addressed me in English. 'Are you a friend of Migumi?'

'Yes, that's right. I haven't heard from her for several days and I was expecting a message.'

'Ah! I understand. She must have left Paris

because of her work. Do you usually deal with her personally?'

'Yes, yes!' I stammered.

'I'm sorry, she hasn't left any message for you. But I can receive you in future. I'll give you my card. From now on, though, you must phone first.'

She took a card from her pocket and gave it to me. I didn't have a chance to say anything. She continued, 'Undoubtedly, you know all about the possibilities of such rendezvous. This card will give you an idea of the prices and services.'

I cast a quick glance at it, then said, 'And Misako?'

'Ah! Misako left with Migumi. They won't be back for a long time.'

'Can you tell me where they've gone?'

'They'll be travelling a lot, so I can't give you an address. I'm sorry, but I've got to go now. But ring me if you require my services. Good night.'

I went away feeling perplexed. The card was still in my hand and I began to read it. Her name was printed on it, together with times and prices . . .

I returned home and threw the card on my desk, on top of all the letters and papers. I wondered what had really happened to

Migumi and what had caused such a precipitate departure. I lost myself in a maze of conjectures, each one madder than the others.

One thing was certain. Migumi worked on a razor's edge. The development of her agency depended upon a cleverly organised call-girl network – supplied by her own mannequins. Undoubtedly, that made business run more smoothly on an international scale.

My indiscreet curiosity had led Misako to let me into the secret. Migumi found out and had undoubtedly brought about this abrupt end to our relationship.

For three months or more, I had been the partner of those two superb and mysterious Japanese women. I was the fortunate chosen participant in an exceptional lovers' contract. They had never made me feel ashamed of my desires. Migumi had taught me a whole erotic art. Never before had I experienced such hot nights as those which I spent with her. What could I infer from this sudden disappearance?

I spent that night of revelation recalling all the places where we had met, all those scenes of burning eroticism, all the circumstances in which I had made love with her, as well as with Misako. My sex stood up again, I was waiting for caresses, passionate embraces, infinite sucking. All that happened was that I wore myself out and dropped off to sleep.

The next day, I tidied up the papers which covered my desk. What a mess! I found a postcard there with a picture of an island on it. It was from a girlfriend informing me that she was on her way home. I looked at the date absently.

I decided to start living my life again, to forget my nights with Migumi. But would it be possible?

I spent the rest of the day in a recording-studio. Things went very well. I returned home at eight, full of good humour. I poured myself a generous Martini.

Suddenly the telephone rang. For a moment memories crowded in upon me. I went over and picked up the receiver with a strange feeling of foreboding.

It was Eurielle, who had just returned from the Bahamas.

Her voice was gorged with sunshine. I had met her at a cocktail-party which was being given to celebrate the release of her first record. As well as being a singer, she was an actress. I had taken her from her producer, the evening of our first meeting, not without causing some trouble. And with the passage of time, we had remained lovers.

'Well, well! At least you're alive,' she said. 'I sent you three letters in which I suggested you should come and join me, if you could get away

207

from the studio.'

'I'm sorry, Eurielle, but I haven't been opening my post lately. I've been having a torrid affair.'

'Have you found another singer?'

'No, not really. But she knew how to pluck her "Lute Chords".'

'What are you talking about?'

'She was Japanese and believe me . . .'

Eurielle wouldn't let me go on. 'And what was so special about her? Have you forgotten our nights together?'

'Ah, if only you knew! Sometimes there were several of them serving me!'

'Try to be more explicit, please!'

I told Eurielle what had happened to me with Migumi and Misako and about the multiple facets of the Japanese art of eroticism practised according to traditional rules. I also referred to the contract which had bound me to them and the acrobatic feats I had performed during all those nights.

Eurielle became excited. She could contain herself no longer. 'I want you to be the "Phoenix in My Scarlet Ravine!" You bastard, I'm coming over, now!'

Then I felt as if my stalk was gorged with sunshine.